A NEW Game

A MMF Erotic Romance

NOA ROSE

A NEW GAME

For information contact :
http://www.tamingchaos.net

Interior design by Chaos Publications
Cover design by Black Bird Covers

ISBN: 9 7 8 1 9 5 4 4 1 3 0 8 5
1st Edition: October 2022

Chaos
PUBLICATIONS

This book was written to prove that I could
step out of my comfort zone.
Look at me go!

And, for my beta readers, Andrew, Anne,
Brad C., Brad L., Brian, Ceasar, Christina,
Clara, Jennifer, Kelsey, and Matt C.
Thank you for stepping out of *your* comfort
zones.

01

A light breeze swirled its way down the narrow streets of downtown Alexandria. It created a song in the leaves on the characteristic cherry blossom trees that were so notable in the spring. Soft pink blossoms floated down onto the patrons of the weekend farmer's market, like snow falling in winter. They littered the ground, turning everything pink for the season that drew so many tourists to the DC area. Angel Rivera loved when the cherry blossoms were in full bloom. It made everything in his home town seem magical.

"No! Ugh! Angel, will you tell this lady I don't want the whole box? I want individual fruits! *Uno!*"

The magic shattered, replaced by Angel's roommate and the man's inability to people. Quinn Lang looked at him desperately, holding up one bright red apple in one hand, while gesturing at the vendor with the other. The woman was of Latin descent. She'd been selling at the farmer's market for years, and was one of Angel's favorite people. She also had a wicked sense of humor and liked to tease Quinn when he came out by *only* speaking Spanish. The woman was fluent in four different languages, including English.

Angel smiled, speaking to the vendor in Spanish to appease Quinn. He paid for half a dozen apples, thanked her for the fruit, and the midday amusement, before handing the canvas sack to his disgruntled roommate.

"You could have just held up fingers," Angel teased lightly, elbowing Quinn in the arm. The frumpy programmer merely rubbed his arm where Angel bumped him and pouted.

"Why am I out here with you? Where's Rachel? This is usually her thing, not mine. You people with her and play video games with me. That's how it's always been, Angel. You can't change things on me like this! I don't like surprises."

"It isn't a surprise, Quinn. I go to the farmer's market every Saturday," Angel said, throwing a winning smile at his roommate.

"With *Rachel*," Quinn countered. "Is she taking a break from playing work wife or something?"

"Yes. I chose angsty Quinn to play the game of life with me today," Angel teased. Quinn did not seem amused.

Angel didn't let Quinn's sour mood ruin the day. He stopped at nearly every stall and vendor, picked up things for his sisters, mom, and his cousins, got some new plants for the apartment, and even bought Quinn a little succulent to go next to his desk. Now he'd have a little bit of greenery to look at, while he worked in the cave he insisted on inhabiting. By the time they got back to their shared apartment, Quinn was in better spirits, proudly proclaiming that the succulent would now be called Juju-Bean in honor of the cat he'd always wanted as a child but never got.

"Promise I don't have to go with you to the farmer's market next weekend," Quinn said from his room before coming out in a pair of threadbare sweats and a tee-shirt so old it looked two sizes too small for him. Angel merely blinked at him. "What?"

"Had that shirt since junior high, have we?" Angel mocked. Quinn looked down at the shirt, then threw a glower at Angel. Angel merely laughed at Quinn's inability to play the game of life.

The two met in college as assigned roommates in their freshman year at George

Mason University. They drifted apart after that first year, until grad school, when chance brought them together again. They'd stayed in contact, hanging out when time and social calendars allowed. They would meet up with their own circle of friends until those circles merged together, and eventually dwindled to a small handful of mutual acquaintances that got together for beer pong and darts. After graduation, adulting became the name of the game. Friends moved away, married, had children, or took darker paths along life's narrow alleys that, to this day, Angel did not like thinking about. It was during those times that Quinn proposed a split on a place in Rock Creek. That was where they went, and where they stayed going on six long years now.

Angel was roughly eighteen months older than Quinn. It stood out when they first met and continued to rule their relationship. Angel took care of Quinn because that was what older people were *supposed* to do in Angel's mind. Quinn was smart, graduating high school two years early and taking a weird six-month something-or-other in Ireland that he *still* complained about. The man was a walking enigma, but Angel loved him all the same.

Life just wouldn't be the same without Quinn.

#

By Sunday evening, the farmer's market fiasco was but a distant memory. Quinn rolled his neck, hearing it crack, before wiping the steam from the bathroom mirror. He was not looking forward to the start of the work week. There was a big project due that he'd put off, and now he felt the anxiety and panic gnawing at his gut like some weird parasite waiting to burst out of his stomach. In the back of his mind, he heard Angel's voice chiding him for procrastinating so much, grinning to himself as he opened the bathroom door, only to stop dead in his tracks.

Angel did pushups on the living room floor, bare back glistening with sweat. It brought the angel wings tattooed on his skin into stark focus. They started at his shoulder blades, stretching across his back and down his upper arms. Just above and between the wings was a Mayan ouroboros with a single date inside of it – the day Angel died.

Quinn knew the story, had heard it recounted millions of times at get-togethers with Angel's family. His *abuelita* would tell it like a miracle from God Himself that her grandson returned to them after an accident that nearly took his life. *Did* take his life – for thirty-eight terrifying minutes. They counted every day since as a blessing, and prayed for him at every meal. The first couple times Quinn heard it, it felt weird. Now it was as easy for him to pray for his friend as it was for him to curse at his screen. Watching Angel workout always seemed to make Quinn squirm, however.

"You're... sweating all over the floor," Quinn croaked, making sure to hold tight to the towel draped over his shoulder.

"So?" Angel replied through heavy breaths as he continued his reps. "You sweat on the couch all the time. I don't complain."

"No, you Febreeze it," Quinn shot back. He heard Angel laugh, watching as his roommate stopped and rolled onto his back instead. He had his long hair tied back in a tail, the gold cross at his neck falling to the side. The man had more tattoos on his chest, each of them significant in one way or another. He had the Japanese symbols for love and faith on the inside of each wrist, and a rather intricate tree of life on his chest, a chest that also glistened with sweat. Quinn just made a face at Angel and looked at the floor rather than stare at his roommate.

"Whatever. Now that you're out of the shower, I'll go get clean so I don't sweat on the floor that *I* mop," Angel teased, rising to his feet.

"Excuse me, Mo the Mop cleans the floor,"

Quinn corrected, looking over to the set of machines just beneath their fish tank that mopped and vacuumed, respectively. Angel glanced at them, then back at Quinn with an arched brow.

"Fine, next time I'll just sweat in my room," he said, then *pranced* into the bathroom. *Pranced!*

Life was certainly not dull with Angel in it. In fact, Quinn knew how lost he'd be without Angel, and dreaded the day he'd no longer be there, much like he dreaded his upcoming presentation. Sadly, Monday came all too soon for the gamer recluse.

"Angel! Do you know where my keys are!" Quinn called as he dug through the pile of crap stacked, two deep, on his desk. His presentation was in an hour. He'd forgotten about how early it was until Angel reminded him by wishing him luck for the thing at breakfast. Quinn scheduled things for after noon for a reason!

"On the hook where they always are," Angel said as he walked by Quinn's door to his own room. Quinn muttered to himself, throwing two thin binders and a handful of papers into his backpack, along with his laptop. He grabbed his phone, stuffed his feet into his shoes and nearly collided with Angel on his way to the door.

"Jesus, Angel!" Quinn cursed.

"Don't take the Lord's name in vain, Q,"

Angel said. He always said that. He didn't go to church like his mom and *abuelita* did, but he prayed every night, and crossed himself every morning before he set foot out the door for work.

"Don't step out in front of me like a ninja," Quinn countered. Angel merely shook his head, moving into the kitchen without a single worry in the world. "Do you know where the extra–"

"Here," Angel said, already pulling the extra Metro card out of the kitchen drawer where all the miscellaneous things lived. Angel knew where everything was, even if that something existed inside the drawer that was known as a home's black hole.

For the most part, their apartment was well-organized and as immaculate as a bachelor pad could be. Angel liked to keep things clean and sorted. There was a calendar on the fridge with every appointment, event, or due date imaginable. There was a tiny composting machine next to the cleaning bots, recycling bins divided by type, and a label maker to date the left-overs. Things still got messy though. Sometimes the trash didn't go out on time, or the pizza boxes got left on the coffee table after game night, but Angel was a meticulous person. He followed his routine and kept things tidy.

Quinn, on the other hand, was a chaos engine.

The video game developer lived out of the same hamper for over two weeks at a time. His desk was a riot of papers and granola bar wrappers, despite having a trash bin right beneath his desk. He wore the same four things over and over, and didn't have anything fancier than a pair of jeans and a single button-down shirt. The only 'routine' he had was to fap it out once or twice during his six o'clock meetings out of sheer boredom.

"Thank you," Quinn said, snatching the Metro card from Angel's hands before dashing out the door, already wishing for a do-over to the week before it had even started.

02

By mid-week, the stress of having to actually be social during the weekend, and the crazy start to the actual week was weighing heavily on Quinn. He squinted at the screen in front of him before comparing it to another screen to his left. He had one more on the desk, and two mounted above his work station. Each had a purpose, each one engaging part of his attention with various stimuli so he could actually get his work done. His leg bounced in agitation as he tried to match the code with the motions of the high-definition character on the left. He had deliverables due soon, even if those deliverables were virtual. Games still had specific release dates. Producers got cranky when the prime NPC of the game slashed instead of stabbed.

The light in his apartment grew dim, making the colors on the screen wash him out. He ignored the calls that came through, silencing his phone. He barely remembered to use the bathroom, working in his pajamas since breakfast. When the phone buzzed its way across his desk after several hours of silence, he jumped, cursing when the involuntary reflex made him hit the enter key one too many times, ruining the line of code he was working on.

"Speak," he answered, hitting the speaker button without even looking. He did that often. Angel warned him against it, saying that one day it would be some Nigerian prince with a million dollars if Quinn would just give him his routing number and that Quinn would be so distracted he would just give the number up. If Angel only knew.

"Wow, busy?" Angel said on the other end. Hearing his voice immediately relieved some of the tension Quinn felt in his shoulders and neck, even if he remained hunched over his keyboard like the basement troll he really was.

"Working," Quinn replied in a curt tone. His eyes narrowed, fingers moving over the keys to correct the mistake.

"Have you even eaten today? Or pissed in a toilet?" Angel asked. He always asked questions like that. Sometimes it was cute, most times it was annoying. Angel naturally took on the role of caretaker. He'd done it in college and continued to do it now. Twelve years ago, Quinn did not appreciate vegetables as much as he did now. Angel's persistence allowed Quinn to appreciate vegetables more, especially now, when his stomach growled loudly at him. He would kill to have Angel shove a plate of carrot sticks in his face, even if he would not admit it to the other man over the phone.

"I had ramen," Quinn lied. He hadn't eaten anything. "So, I'll see you tomorrow?"

"I haven't even said why I'm calling," Angel quipped. Quinn snorted. "Don't snort at me. Why do you always assume it's for the same reason?"

"Because it's Wednesday. You always 'stay late' on Wednesday. You're like a clock, Angel. Very punctual."

"You suck, you know that?"

Quinn smirked. "Yeah, whatever. Tell Rachel to send you back in one piece this time. Laundry isn't really my thing. Bring me donuts tomorrow," Quinn said, hanging up without further fanfare. Angel didn't *have* to call Quinn. Quinn was well aware of what Angel was doing when he didn't come home – or rather, *whom*. Rachel was Angel's 'work wife'. They had some sort of friends-with-benefits relationship going. Quinn tried not to question it too much. Relationships were not Quinn's strong suit. He created magnificent code, could name every superhero and their powers, he even made a decent cauliflower pizza, but relationships stumped him every time.

Shaking his head at his predictable friend, Quinn turned his attention back to work. "Ok, mister swordsmith, I need you to–" Quinn started, cutting off with a choking sound when the doorbell rang. "Seriously? What is with today?"

First all the calls, then Angel, now the doorbell. He hadn't even ordered dinner yet. Quinn growled and grumbled as he went to the door, tripping over the edge of the rug that he *always* tripped over. Angel had once suggested they just get rid of the rug so it would stop sneak–attacking Quinn at all hours of the day. Quinn argued that it filled the day with unwanted but amusing surprises. The surprise at the door was worse than a stealth rug.

"Mom," he screeched when he saw her standing in the hallway with his father looming above her, fake smiles plastered to their faces.

#

Angel looked at his phone, then chuckled as his co–worker sidled up to him with a cold beer and a brilliant smile. She had a more distinct look to her than most women in DC, with long brown hair, luscious curves and a round, cute face that drew attention to her beautiful green eyes. On any given day, she might be missed in a crowd, passed over on the Metro, even ignored while she raced through Capitol Hill. But she'd caught Angel's eye, enough to get them talking. An incident on the Metro brought them closer together as he was the one to defend her against the jerk that thought to get too fresh with a nice-looking woman during the late-night runs on the train. Angel had been dozing when Rachel screeched at someone to leave her alone. The fool of a man got up off the floor three stops after Angel and Rachel departed, with a broken nose and two black eyes.

Three years later, nothing had changed between them. He still defended her against the jerks that believed women were the lesser of the sexes, made sure she was safe at night before heading home, and met her every morning so she never had to ride the Metro alone again. They'd grown closer, trusted each other implicitly, had steady trysts with each other, and enjoyed rom-com movie marathons together. It was simple, no-strings intimacy that they could not find anywhere else.

"And how is your house husband doing today?" Rachel smiled. Angel chuckled. If Rachel was his 'work wife', the running joke among their mutual friends was that Quinn was his 'house husband'. The man worked primarily from home, but that was where the 'house' part of the description ended. If Angel didn't set the reminders on Quinn's phone himself, the man would never remember to eat, let alone do any other household type chore. Angel did most of the chores anyway, as he was very meticulous about how things should be. Quinn never cared enough to argue against how Angel did things. So long as the other man did the dishes from time to time, Angel was fine with their unique lifestyle. Quinn offered a different kind of intimacy – the kind that let you use the toilet while someone else showered.

"Fighting with code again, sounded like. Which means he's got something due this week, and he put it off," Angel said, taking a drink from his beer before leaning down to give Rachel a kiss. She purred back at him, wrapping her arms loosely around his neck.

"Someone's in a mood," she smiled. He rarely initiated sex with her. They maintained their weekly trysts out of both habit and a need for companionship. He was always happy to simply exist in her presence, never pressuring her into anything. They got together on Saturdays for the farmer's market, and every Wednesday night, but that didn't mean they were always intimate. Sometimes, it was just nice to cuddle on a couch that didn't smell like pizza.

"Maybe a little," he rumbled in return.

The beers were forgotten after that, both of them stripping each other of their work clothing and tossing it aside like discarded trash. Angel put his hands all over Rachel's curves, kissing her neck and shoulder, running his fingers through her hair until they were both breathing so hard one might think they were about to hyperventilate.

"Lie back," Rachel breathed, pushing Angel back onto the soft leather sofa in their shared office space. He complied, smiling at her as she kissed her way down his chest, nosing at the base of his cock in a seductive tease that had him hard in no time. She sucked him off slowly, enjoying it, drawing it out until she was satisfied with her work, then crawled back up his now very tense body. She positioned him at her entrance and slid down his length until he was seated to the hilt.

"God, Rae," he breathed out, taking her by her rounded hips as she rode him through to her first orgasm. She continued, adding a little bounce to her undulating hips that had Angel groaning. His hands caressed her sides and back while he took a breast into his mouth. Hearing her moan made him growl and move with her until she was bouncing from tip to base.

"Oh, God, Angel!" she panted, head thrown back. He loved when she screamed his name. He loved it more when he screamed *hers*. She'd once given him a massage so sensual he orgasmed twice before they even had sex. "Angel!"

She cried his name as she orgasmed again. Her fingers dug into his chest, scratching him while she continued to bounce hard on his cock until he literally exploded. Their love making slowed down after that, becoming something more calm and sensual until they both had weak muscles and sore bellies.

"Marry me," she said to him afterwards as they lay on the floor together beneath a soft sherpa blanket. She rested against his chest while he ran fingers through her hair. Her fingers traced the edges of the tattoo on his chest, winding along every curve and bend in the intricate tree. They both stared out the floor–to–ceiling window in their office overlooking Farragut Square.

"What?" he asked, feeling a little knot form in his stomach. This was not how their relationship worked. It was casual, easy, no strings trust. Rachel giggled.

"Not now, silly. I don't want anything now. You don't either. But, I dunno, when we're old. Like... forty-five. If we haven't found anyone by then, marry me. I don't want to be alone when I'm older, you know?"

Angel thought about what she said. He'd just turned thirty-two. Rachel was two years his senior, so there would need to be technical discussions regarding age, but he didn't see any fault in what she was asking. He didn't want to live his life alone, either. And, while he was not in any rush, he knew it would come up sooner or later. His parents and *abuelita* asked him any time he went home when he would give them grandchildren. He wasn't ready for kids. He knew that was part of why he trusted Rachel so much – she couldn't have children. He never asked why and did not think less of her for it, like others might. Intimacy did not equate to baby making in his mind. He could easily see growing old with Rachel, and smiled down at her.

"Sure," he said. "I'll marry you."

"Really?" she smiled. He nodded at her, giving her a sweet kiss. She mewled against his lips, then laughed as she pulled back. "Who gets to tell Quinn?"

03

Angel shut his eyes as the Metro rumbled along beneath downtown DC toward his condo in Rock Creek. He liked the respite that using public transportation gave him as well as knowing he was doing his part to keep another gas-guzzling car off the roads – – especially in DC. Quinn would be home, probably in his boxers, yelling at his work station because, unlike Angel, Quinn didn't work like normal people. They both had good-paying jobs, and both enjoyed the type of work they did, but Quinn got to do what he loved in his boxers while Angel had to wear a suit and tie half the time. Angel lobbied for climate change and animal rights; Quinn *lobbed* magic spells at people, then cursed at the screen when the code to make such a thing possible created a glitch that took him five hours to work out. Different jobs, different stresses, but an otherwise comfortable existence.

He thought about Rachel's proposal until the Metro came to a stop for him to disembark. He wondered, sometimes, if Rachel was ok at night, alone in her apartment with her attack chihuahua. It was a tiny, useless thing that was as fierce as any pitbull Angel had ever seen. He still had the scars to prove it, too. But, clearly, it did not provide the same sort of companionship she yearned for. If it did, she wouldn't have asked Angel to marry her. Except, Angel wasn't really lonely. He just didn't know how to explain that to her without crushing her loving heart.

It was a problem for another day. He waved at the lady that lived two floors down as he checked the day's mail. She was older, another lobbyist like he was, though he didn't know who she worked for, or even her name. All he knew was how she eyeballed Quinn anytime the demi-god of game coding showed his face to the outside world. Quinn wasn't a bad-looking man – for a basement goblin. It was a constant source of ribbing for Angel to toss Quinn's way. He needed sun, needed a diet that had more greens and less freeze-dried noodles and, more importantly, needed to get laid.

"What's-her-face is downstairs if you wanna... go... say... Are you setting the table?"

Angel asked as he entered the large condo on the top floor with the pristine view of Rock Creek Park. Quinn moved around the table, adjusting things to be just so while fighting with the buttons on a shirt that looked like it lost the battle with an iron. "What happened to your shirt?"

"I ironed it," Quinn huffed.

"With what, a blowtorch?" Angel asked, setting his stuff down near the door. There was a shoe rack, coat hooks on the wall, and an armory of Nerf weapons that were often used for stress release and epically childish battles of darts and foam swords. Angel removed his shoes, then watched Quinn with an arched brow and a box of donuts in his hands as requested.

"Funny. Can you go find me a different one? Or can I just borrow one of yours or something?"

"Why? What are you doing?"

"Setting the table. My parents are coming over."

Angel blinked. He'd never met Quinn's parents. He'd known the man for *twelve years* and never once met his parents in person. He'd said hello to them over the phone, and sent them Christmas cards, but the couple lived out in Washington *state* and traveled out of country more often than Angel ate off the food trucks downtown — which was to say, all the time.

"Like... your actual parents?" Angel asked. Quinn huffed at him again, raking a hand through dull black hair that bounced right back to stand on end for a moment before falling back down the middle, splitting on either side of his round face.

"No, asshole, my fake parents," Quinn growled. "Yes, my actual parents!"

Angel chortled, taking a bit of delight in seeing his normally laid back, apathetic roommate so out of sorts. Angel was the one always worrying about things, making sure bills got paid on time, groceries were all within their expiration dates, recycling got sorted correctly, and the lights all got turned off at night. He'd even bought an inside composting machine that Quinn said looked like an alien escape pod.

"Ok, stop," Angel said, setting the donuts down before taking Quinn by the shoulders so he wouldn't grind a ring into their table by shifting the plates around too much. Quinn made a face that was a cross between Kermit the Frog and a child about to throw a tantrum. "First, you definitely need a new shirt, and we will just... God, we can't even donate this one. Ok, so we'll do something with it later. Second, I assume they're coming for dinner?" Quinn nodded. "And what are we feeding them?"

"Dim sum. It'll be here now–ish. I'm not that stupid."

"Ok," Angel laughed. "Then go find a shirt and stop freaking out. It's just your parents. It's about time I met them. How long have I known you?"

"Uhm, about that," Quinn started as he unbuttoned his shirt to a certain point, then just tugged it over his head. Despite his at–home habits and work, he maintained a decent enough physique. They both did. They were both too nerdy to get laid otherwise. "I need you to do me a big, and I mean huge, favor."

"Ok..."

"Just go along with what I say, ok?" Angel blinked and frowned just as the doorbell rang. "Goddammit, of course they're early. Stall them!"

Quinn darted toward Angel's bedroom, making Angel's frown deepen as he went to the door. It was the delivery guy. Angel accepted the food, took it to the kitchen and put it on serving plates, when the doorbell rang again.

"Answer it!" Quinn hissed, sticking his head out of the door long enough to do so before darting back into the room. Angel merely shook his head and looked at the door. Quinn was going to have a coronary before his parents even set foot in the door at the rate he was going. But

Angel was nothing if not punctual, so he tucked a long lock of brown hair behind his ear and walked to the door.

"Hi, you must be Quinn's parents," he said as he stared at a couple that was so White Bread American, Angel nearly let his jaw hit the floor. Quinn was Asian. "I'm Angel."

"Well, you're just nothing like Quinn's described," Quinn's mother said, coming in without accepting Angel's extended hand. Angel tried not to take offense, wondering how Quinn was describing him to his parents. Quinn's father snorted and followed his wife.

"Please, make yourselves at home," Angel managed, mentally cursing at them in Spanish for their poor manners.

"I told you it was a cute little place to live. It's got a great view. What's the rent here?" Quinn's mother asked. She looked like she just stepped off the cover of *Glamour* magazine. Everything was perfectly pressed and perfectly coifed. Angel could not, for the life of him, remember her name other than 'Mrs. Lang'. She surveyed Rock Creek Park from the dining-room window while Quinn's father sneered at the pictures on the wall.

They were all of Quinn and Angel doing Quingel things. That was the mash-up name their friends gave them. There was a sweaty picture at the basketball courts, and a picture of them with their larger group of friends. There was another of them being stupid and posing beneath the bronze bull on Wallstreet, and another still of them at the Bean in Chicago. Neither of them had time for significant others. Most of the time, women just complicated life to an extreme that neither man was prepared for. Quinn's last girlfriend was when they were still in college to Angel's last recollection, and Angel's last girlfriend threatened to stab him with her stiletto for trying to educate another woman on the importance of reusable straws. They'd only dated a month before that happened. He'd just plain given up after that and called it a sign from God. Rachel was good enough for him.

"Hey!" Quinn said as he came out wearing one of Angel's shirts, tight jeans that were also probably from Angel's closet, given their excess length, and no shoes.

"Quinn!" the parents said in unison, doting upon him like he was three. And Angel thought *his* family was bad. They gave him hugs, but none of it seemed real. It just seemed rehearsed, like something they'd done so often it had become habit.

"Quinn Anthony, where are your shoes?" Mrs. Lang asked. Angel made a mental note to store Quinn's middle name away for future use.

"We're in the house," he replied simply. "Angel says it tracks in foreign organisms from outside."

Both Langs looked at their feet, then at Angel. He'd said no such thing and frowned at Quinn, who threw him a warning look. Angel merely wiggled his toes in his mismatched socks.

Dinner finally came and went. Angel watched Quinn pick at his dinner while the Langs filled the silence with conversation. They liked to talk about themselves; a lot. They listed all the places they'd been recently, the way the family business was going and the deals that were coming down the pipeline. Angel did not catch what it was, exactly, that Mr. Lang did, but it was, apparently, quite lucrative. By dessert he wanted to bash Quinn over the head with a beer bottle for putting him through this crap. The pair were rude, judgmental, and as fake as the 'Spanish' tile in the bathroom.

"So, Quinn, your mother and I wanted to ask what's going on with you two," Mr. Lang began. "Your birthday's coming up pretty quick, sport."

"Yeah, I know," Quinn nodded, speaking in a tone that sounded defeated. Angel glanced at his roommate, then Mr. Lang. Quinn was not the most social creature on the planet, but he was never one to sound defeated unless he was trying to buy apples at the Farmer's Market. When he suddenly reached for Angel's hand under the table, Angel looked down before thinking, then back up again, hoping no one had noticed. He was, sadly, disappointed. Mrs. Lang looked at him like a shark that caught the scent of blood in the water. Suddenly, the 'go with it' started to come through whatever dinner haze Angel was floating on until that moment. "Look, guys, there's been something I wanted to tell you for a while now..."

Oh, he is not... Angel mentally groaned, mouth going dry and stomach churning.

"You're gay," Mrs. Lang interrupted. "We know, pumpkin."

"Wait, what?" Angel blurted before he could catch himself. He was glad to hear the same echo in Quinn following his voice.

"You... knew?" Quinn dared.

"Oh, Quinn, I've known you were gay since middle school. Honestly, it was the only outcome. There isn't a woman alive that would want the package you're carrying," Mrs. Lang chortled. Angel's chest tightened and his eyes clouded with red. Quinn merely looked down at his plate of half-eaten dim sum.

"I'm sorry, what *package* isn't what women would want?" Angel dared. Quinn dug his fingernails into Angel's hand.

"Quinn's never been very physically attractive, Angel. He's always been quieter and more withdrawn than other boys," Mrs. Lang explained, as if being shy was a crime. Angel wanted to throttle her. "Honestly, it's a wonder he attracted *you*."

"Mom!" Quinn barked, squeezing harder on Angel's hand to stop him from flying across the table like he wanted to. Quinn's leg bounced so much it was a wonder the whole apartment didn't shake. "Angel and I *are* engaged. Just… we haven't said anything because we thought… I dunno… and Angel's family…"

"Doesn't know yet. I haven't decided how to tell them. There's a lot of them and if I tell one over the other first, they'll start a war with each other over who I like better," Angel lied. Well, it was almost a lie. He had to tell his mother first, his Tia Lucia second, and then his sister, Leti. After that, the family gossip chain took care of itself.

Silence. The Langs merely stared.

"So, you're getting married?" Mr. Lang asked.

"Eventually, dad, we aren't in any real rush. We only just got engaged."

"You've lived together for six years," Mr. Lang crowed. "What the hell have you been waiting for? It's time to man up, Quinn, and do what needs to be done."

"Larry!" Mrs. Lang warned. Angel wanted to groan. He could not fathom any reason for Quinn to suddenly need to lie to his parents *about being gay* and *engaged*. More specifically *with Angel.* Their opinions made him want to scream. The way they treated Quinn made him want to stab them with the fork on his plate!

"Quinn, you know what needs to be done. If you want your inheritance, you have to be married. You're running out of time, son."

"Larry, stop. Leave the boy alone. Just be happy you don't have to go beg Maxie for that favor," Mrs. Lang said.

"Dad, seriously?" Quinn said, clearly affronted, though the reasoning was entirely lost on Angel. It was like these people were speaking Greek. It was worse than Greek; it was 'rich'.

The fact that Angel was only learning about all of this *now* while under intense scrutiny and pressure only made his blood pressure intensify. He held Quinn's hand with an iron grip, feeling some of the muscles spasm as a warning of a coming seizure. He forced himself to breathe calmly, to finish the meal in silence, and let Quinn argue with his parents over when and where to have their supposed wedding.

Mrs. Lang was already insisting on hosting the wedding at the country club near their home in Puget Sound and letting Bella — whoever that was — coordinate the event. Quinn did his best to not look like he'd eaten a sour lemon while he listened to his parents plan out a wedding that technically should not have even been a topic of conversation. Quinn was so incensed about the whole thing that Angel was the one to see them out, listening when he caught part of their conversation as they walked to the elevator.

"I told you he was gay. You should have made it clear from the beginning that it wouldn't be a problem, Larry."

"When did I say it wouldn't be a problem, Marjorie? I might ask Maxie for a favor, anyway. This is ridiculous. He doesn't even eat meat."

"Oh, stop it! You're just being…"

Angel shut the door after that, feeling rage roil in his gut. He wasn't sure if it was at Larry Lang or Quinn, or both, but Quinn was who he saw first. Angel's fist flew before he could stop himself, connecting sharply with Quinn's jaw. He didn't like admitting to his foul temper and tried to keep his stress levels in check for health reasons, but this was about to make him blow several gaskets and the pent-up rage had to go somewhere. Quinn just made it too convenient.

"Jesus Christ, Angel!" Quinn cursed, holding the spot where Angel's hand connected. He had a hard head. Angel's hand hurt. He shook it out and walked to his room, slamming the door shut. "Angel!"

"Engaged!" Angel roared, ripping the door open again. Quinn stumbled backwards, falling on his ass. "We're *engaged*, Quinn! We're not even *gay!*"

"I can explain, but you need to stop trying to hit me!" Quinn flinched. Angel stopped, fist raised mid-air. Instead, he folded his arms across his chest, nostrils flaring, and waited. He couldn't afford a seizure now, so Angel forced his temper back into its secret box where it belonged. "Ok, I'll be honest, I thought you were going to keep hitting me."

"ARGH!" Angel roared and stormed back into his room, slamming the door a second time.

04

Quinn very pointedly stayed out of Angel's way over the next two days until the weekend forced them to be in close proximity to each other. Angel refused to come out of his room. He felt betrayed, used, furious. Hell, he hadn't even known Quinn was *adopted*. Quinn Lang was the chubby Filipino kid everyone picked on their freshman year of college; the kid that spent most of his spare time designing phone games, and the rest of his time in the gym with Angel so people would stop calling him 'tubby'. They ate ramen out of the cup and spent long nights in the computer lab hosting World of Warcraft tournaments with the rest of the geeks and nerds on campus. The guy hovering at his bedroom door was someone Angel didn't know at all.

"Angel?"

Angel lobbed a baseball at the door to get Quinn's face off the other side of it. He'd told Rachel what happened. The only reason he wasn't staying with her was because she thought the entire situation was hilarious. Angel didn't want to talk to *her* either.

"Oh, come on! You can't stay in there forever! You haven't even eaten today! You love Saturdays! It's farmer's market day!"

Angel glowered more, finding a nearby shoe to lob since the baseball rolled away from Angel's considerably sized bed.

Angel had a simple existence. He went to work, fought for change in the world, worked out daily, recycled, kept track of what he ate, and made sure he called his insanely large family at least once a week to catch up on gossip. He went out to clubs sometimes, watched horror movies on Fridays and football on Sundays like any good American did. Whatever bullshit Quinn was trying to pull, Angel wanted none of it.

"I'm sorry I didn't warn you before. They showed up Wednesday night when you were with Rachel! I had to tell them something! They asked where you were. I told them you were working late! Honestly, they could've caught me with my hand down my pants!"

"Cuz that would have gone *so well* for your little story! Stop masturbating during your six o'clock meetings, Quinn! You were supposed to be working anyway!" Angel barked back. "God, is this what you've been telling them the whole fucking time! That we live together cuz we're *gay*!"

"No! They just … assumed… "

Angel threw his other shoe at the door. He watched Quinn's feet move back a step or two, then shift back so he could see Quinn's heels. There was the distinct sound of someone sliding against the bedroom door. Angel could see the rounded outline of Quinn sitting on the floor just beneath the door.

"In case it wasn't obscenely obvious, I'm adopted," Quinn began. Angel threw a flat glare at his door. "Don't glare at me. I didn't choose my parents. They chose me. It's what they do. Like a weird game of the rich and famous. And they are. Rich, I mean."

Angel snorted. He'd seen the massive diamond ring on Mrs. Lang's finger along with the *other* diamond bands on the rest of her fingers. Mr. Lang wore a Rolex watch and Armani pants. Angel had been around enough senators and lobbyists to know what those things looked like. He wasn't poor by any stretch of the word, but he didn't feel the need to waste money on frivolous things like

Armani suits. There was nothing at all practical about things like that.

Quinn was much the same. He spent his money on ramen subscriptions from Japan and video game paraphernalia. They ate out, bought good bottles of wine, good beer, and lived in the 'yuppie' part of town. Come to think of it, they were kind of like an old married couple. Curse him. How many other people thought they were gay?!

Quinn continued. "I get a monthly allowance from them that's going to stop soon unless..."

"Unless, what? You marry your dad's choice of woman?" Angel scoffed. What fantasy was Quinn living?

"Sort of. *Who* I'm married to wasn't ever clearly stated, just that I be married... *before* I turn thirty. I assumed if I told them I was engaged to a guy that they'd sort of just... I dunno, throw a fit and leave me alone after that. I wasn't expecting them to want me to still get married."

Angel frowned. "Quinn, you turn thirty in October."

Silence.

"It's May," Angel added.

Silence.

Despite not wanting to forgive so quickly, Angel's curiosity got the better of him. He huffed and slid off the bed, opening the door fast enough to knock Quinn off balance. The other man fell back with a thud and a wince, looking up at Angel from the floor.

"You get a fucking *allowance* from your parents every month?" Quinn nodded, silent and on the floor like an overturned turtle. Angel thought on it a little more. "How much money?"

"A lot?"

"Define 'a lot' Quinn. Don't make me use your middle name or get my flip-flop. Do not for one second think I will not give you the *chanclazo* of a lifetime for this bullshit."

Quinn blinked, opened his mouth, then shut it again and remained perfectly still in the doorway of Angel's room as he thought about how to answer the question. Or maybe he was trying to figure out what a *chanclazo* was. Angel was more than happy to demonstrate for him.

"A month? Thirty thousand," Quinn finally sighed. "I'll get one-hundred million once I'm married and the allowance stops."

"Fuck you," Angel said in clear disbelief. Quinn blinked innocently at him. *"De veras?"*

"Don't go all Hispanic on me. You know I failed Spanish in high school," Quinn chuffed. Angel kicked him. "Ow! I never said I wanted the money!"

"Then why does it matter if you're married! Christ, you already *have* the money! You make more in a month sitting on your ass *not* working than most make in a fucking year! Why! Does! It! Matter!" Angel threw back, kicking him again with each word he grunted through clenched teeth. He wasn't wearing shoes, so he knew it didn't hurt nearly as much as Quinn was letting on.

"Because it matters to my dad! I don't know! I panicked, ok! I'm sorry! Didn't you ever wonder why I never let you talk to my parents for long? Or meet them. We've lived together for six years, Angel. I've met every single one of your thirty-seven first cousins and you met my parents two days ago."

Angel twisted his lips in anger and annoyance as he contemplated what Quinn said. Quinn *had* met all of Angel's cousins. He knew Angel's mom and stepdad, his *abuelita*, aunts, uncles, nieces and nephews, his brothers, his half-sisters and step-siblings. Angel's family was loud and brash, in your face, hard-working people that lived across five different states and had ties to every single branch of the military. And now his youngest sister was about to join the Space Force. Angel was one of the few that opted to not go into the armed forces, paying for college with scholarships and part-time jobs so he could be a servant of the people *and* the planet. Literally everyone in his family picked on him for it, but it was what made Angel happy, so it made *them* happy.

Quinn worked for a gaming company. He'd told Angel that he had no siblings, one cousin he didn't like, and a weird hatred of tiny ponies. Except, clearly, all that was wrong. Except, maybe, the ponies; that part might still be true.

"One-hundred *million*?" Angel asked. Quinn sighed and muttered something that could be taken as a positive response. "I want half."

"What?"

"I want half. If you want to save your inheritance and your dignity, with *my help*, then I want half."

"Angel, this isn't a game. Dad won't give me the money if it isn't real. You heard them. They were already planning on letting my sister be the coordinator!"

"Your *sister*?" Angel growled, giving Quinn a good kick again.

"Ow! Stop that!" the other man said, finally rolling up onto all fours so he could stand rather than lie on the floor like a roach. "Yes, my sister. I have... look, we're all adopted. It was like some philanthropic bullshit. We all come from different countries, and we all hated our lives with a purple passion. They will ruin your life, too. Is that worth fifty million?"

"Yes!" Angel screeched. "We can get it annulled after we get the money, but you're damned right it's worth whatever horseshit your psycho family is gonna pull."

"And your family?"

"Gets new houses that they never, ever have to pay for again," Angel pointed out. He would give his family everything he could, his mom and siblings especially. They'd all done so much for him. It was a sentiment that Quinn had seen but never experienced, it seemed. How sad. "So, half and you have to tell my *abuelita* if she finds out. Mom already thinks I'm gay."

"Angel, everyone but Rachel thinks you're gay," Quinn sighed. Angel smacked him on the arm. "Ow, stop! I still have a bruise on my chin from you decking me the other night."

"You deserved it."

"God, how *old* are you?"

"Says the twenty-nine-year-old pouting about inheritance money," Angel threw back. "I want half."

"Are you serious?"

"Are you? Because you have thirty seconds to decide, then I'm slamming my door in your face and packing my things."

"Angel–"

"Twenty–eight, twenty–seven, twenty–six..."

"You're fucking serious. You're being a child right now."

"Nineteen, eighteen..."

"Angel!"

"Thirteen, twelve, eleven, ten, nine, eight..." Quinn gaped at Angel while Angel stared at his watch, counting down the seconds. "Six, five, four, three, two, one."

Angel took hold of his door and swung it as hard as he could toward Quinn.

"Ok, ok, ok!" Quinn squealed, putting his hands out to stop the door. "Half! You get half!"

"Damn right I get half. Ass. Get out of my room."

#

It took over three hours, a beer, and an entire vegetarian pizza, to coax Angel back out of his room. Part of Quinn was absolutely elated at the prospect of being married to Angel, even if it wasn't real. Or, rather, it wasn't meant to last past the required time necessary to gain his inheritance. Despite what others said or how they teased, Quinn *was* gay. He'd had a mad crush on Angel almost since the day they met. From time to time, he caught himself staring a little too long at his roommate. His family situation gave him the necessary skills to hide *a lot*. However, he couldn't hide everything from Angel anymore.

Quinn explained his family in halting detail, starting with their net worth, and going down all their 'philanthropic deeds', including but not limited to the adoption of five children from five different nations. Quinn was the middle child, adopted from the Philippines. His brother Elliott was the eldest, from Egypt; Bella was next. She came from Ukraine, and both were already married. Willow was from India, and Gage was from Columbia. The younger two would need to embark on the same marriage bullshit that Quinn was now embroiled in for their money. Refusal was not an option.

There were other rules and conditions too: no drug addicts, no sex addicts — at least not openly. No gambling problems. No open scandals, having good appearance, reputation, and presentation. They needed to be independently successful, and, until now, of the opposite gender. The way things sounded at dinner, however, that was apparently not an issue.

Quinn would never openly admit it to Angel's face, but the crush he once harbored had become quite an infatuation over the years. Pretending let him live a tiny slice of a wet dream he'd been having since he hit twenty and realized he had no interest in anyone *but* Angel. Angel's initial reaction to things was why Quinn never said anything, happy to maintain the status quo if it meant he could maintain life with Angel at his side. He most definitely didn't expect Angel to go along with it for any reason, money least of all.

Angel was not a money-hungry man. That was part of his allure. He was so incredibly down to earth that it made Quinn want to go save all the whales, plant trees, and come out of the closet all at the same time.

Quinn wanted to say something, to tell Angel his true feelings, but held his tongue. Angel had already experienced so much that one more fucking shoe would bury him for good. Instead, he sat at the bar in silence while Angel went through the motions of his Saturday evening routine to prep dinners for the week, despite missing the weekly farmer's market. He'd already called Rachel, telling her to prep a room just in case.

"You're staring," Angel said while chopping veggies, probably thinking they were all Quinn. It made Quinn shrink into a tighter ball on the bar stool.

"Sorry," Quinn muttered. Angel sighed and set the knife down.

"*Why* are you staring?"

Quinn shrugged. "Just... Angel, are you sure you want to do this? You don't have to. I can just say–"

"Say what, Quinn? Hm? That you lied? That

we're not really engaged? That you're *not* staring at me with puppy dog eyes right now like you want this to actually be a thing? We're not gay. We're doing this because half of one hundred fucking million will let me buy literally everyone in my family a new house that they'll never, ever have to worry about. Otherwise, I'd kick your ass and tell you to get out."

"You can't afford–" Quinn started, ducking when the bowl of summer squash came careening at his head. Angel's temper was not something he found endearing at all. He'd only been on the receiving end of that temper once before. It was an event that landed Quinn in the hospital with wounds from a butcher knife, and Angel in lock–up for the night because their neighbors had called the cops. Angel was normally even–tempered and soft–spoken, but when he was angry, Angel could put a raging rhinoceros to shame. He worked hard at it, not wanting to aggravate his epilepsy that could be triggered by stress. This was stress with a side of headache, topped with agony.

Quinn was about to holler back in defense when Angel's phone rang. Angel glared, then answered the call while Quinn collected the shattered bowl and wet pieces of squash.

"*Que pasa, Leti,*" Angel said, finding something else to chop in a rhythmic fashion.

"Don't you '*que pasa*' me, *pendejo*. You're lucky I'm the only one that checks Facebook on a regular basis, or you'd have a lot more people pissed off at you! Why didn't you call me!" Angel blinked. Leti was his baby sister.

"Uhm... call you about what?" he asked, looking at Quinn, who slowed his motions, feeling his stomach drop.

"Seriously? It is literally all over Facebook right now," Leti continued. Angel threw a flat glare at Quinn, who felt himself shrink as he pulled his phone out to check the aforementioned social media platform. What he saw made him groan while simultaneously making him sick to his stomach.

Quinn's parents – or, more specifically, his mom – made a *huge* deal about their third child's engagement to his long–time roommate all over social media. She positively gushed support for her son's lifestyle and tagged everyone she knew – including Quinn. Luckily, Angel's family didn't use social media too much. Leti, however, was an entirely different story. If *Leti* saw it, their friends were not far behind.

Not five seconds later, Quinn's phone blew up with texts. Too many of those texts started with 'I knew it!' or 'About time!'. Quinn was never one for dating, especially given his hidden preferences.

He'd had a girlfriend or two and felt awkward about it. The rest he chalked up to being a gaming troll, something that everyone could pick on him for. He'd made peace with his lot in life, and now that peace was shattered into tiny pieces, just like the ceramic bowl at his feet.

Leti continued to gab a mile a minute, wanting detail after detail that Angel painstakingly recited, begging her not to tell their extended family or to keep it to a minimum at all costs. He explained why he was doing it, that he was not actually gay, that he would buy her whatever house she wanted (yes, even one on Mars). The call lasted over an hour, leaving Quinn to field all the calls from friends and family that had seen his mother's inappropriate social media post.

By the time it was all over, Quinn wanted to hang himself, and Angel looked decidedly defeated. The other man sat on the sofa with his head draped over the back, eyes closed. He looked exhausted and furious at the same time. It was adorable.

"Angel?" Quinn hazarded. "You, ok?"

Silence.

"Angel?"

"Fine," Angel croaked. Quinn winced.

"I didn't expect things to blow up like this. I'm sorry," Quinn said. Angel cracked an eye open, peering at Quinn with disgust in its brown depth.

"Why did you think something like this *wouldn't* blow up, Quinn?" he muttered.

"I dunno, I didn't think my mom was going to blast our business on social media. She's never cared before."

"Quinn, her *adopted* son is now *engaged* to a *man*. Your mom seems like the type of person to take out space on the billboards across the Nation for something like this because it would get *her* attention."

Angel was not wrong. Marjorie Lang worried about two things: real estate, and reputation. Larry Lang was worse. He was from old money, had never wanted for anything in the world, and insisted on putting those same values on his own children. And now Angel was suffering for it, too. Quinn could see it on his face, catching the slight tremor in his hands.

"You don't have to do this. It won't stop with social media posts," Quinn sighed.

"My mom deserves a better life than what she's got, Quinn," Angel said. He resettled on the sofa and closed his eyes again. Quinn stared at him, looking away quickly when Angel cracked an eye open again.

"You were staring at me. Don't do shit like that. I might get the wrong idea."

Quinn sneered at his friend but shrank down in his seat, fighting down the furious rush of red that was trying to fill his cheeks. He was *not* staring at Angel. Not that he wouldn't if he had the opportunity to do so because Angel was a very handsome man. He had shoulder-length brown hair and a perfect tan with the most adorable smile… No, he was most certainly *not* staring *or* flushing.

"Quinn…"

"What!"

"Seriously, don't get weird on me, ok?"

"Not getting weird."

"You sure?" Angel persisted. Quinn scowled at him. "Ok."

05

"**A**re you fucking kidding me! He's *gay*!" Maximillian Fier sighed, rubbing his temple while his daughter, Racine, raged around the kitchen. Larry had given him the news of his son's engagement to his longtime roommate, something that effectively ended a gentleman's deal they'd made when their two children were still very young: if Quinn was not married on his own by thirty, he would marry Racine. The match was a good one for both families. So far, the elder two Lang children had done the same, marrying members of the community that were of good standing, good stock, and good families. This was... well, unexpected. Racine was less than thrilled.

"Fix this! Fix this right now, daddy! Fix this! That should be *my* wedding and *my* money!"

"Racey, you don't need money, sweet pea," Maximilian sighed. Racine screeched at him like a banshee.

"I want this asshole gone! Dead! Drown him in the Sound if you have to, but get rid of him!" Racine continued.

"Now, sweet pea, that's a bit much, don't you think — thank you, Maria," he said, absently thanking the cook that came around to offer him a stiff drink while cleaning up the things Racine was throwing.

"Fix. This," Racine snarled, leaning over the counter toward her father with a vicious look on her face. "Or I will."

#

Bella Amad sat with back straight and eyebrow arched while her 'bestie' blabbed all about the news circling through the community: Bella's *brother* was gay. The woman had gone down the list of how unfair it was for the middle Lang to get away with being a 'homo' and all manner of horrible things that no sane person would say in public. But they weren't *in* public. They were at high tea with the other community hens, as was expected of them every other Sunday.

"Jessica, please remember you're talking about *my* brother," Bella finally cut in. Jessica turned red. The other ladies at their table snickered softly under their breaths and white gloves. Jessica recovered quickly.

"Oh, come on, Bells, you can't tell me you're not just a little bit annoyed that Q gets to live a fairy tale. Racine is *furious*. I heard from Abigail Dower that…"

Bella tuned Jessica out again. To the outside world, the society in which Bella existed got everything they wanted. They *were* the fairy tale: rich, beautiful, handsome, successful – everything normal people wanted. The reality was not quite as full of glitter and rainbows as everyone liked to think. Fairy tales didn't really exist in their world. Not usually. Sometimes it did, and that person was swiftly ostracized from the community for their happiness. She'd seen it happen to another member of the community who chose to marry someone they met in college, someone they loved and cherished rather than the person their parents arranged for them to marry. It caused a rift between child and parent, and left them out of the community for good. People whispered about them now, wondering if the same would happen to Quinn.

"Excuse me," she said quietly as she stood from her chair. The ladies at the table all watched her leave, whispering furiously at her back. Not even her children were this bad, and they were awful. She reached the car, allowing the driver to open the door for her with a muttered thank you.

"Retail therapy, mum?" the man said in a crisp British lilt. She nodded, giving him a gentle smile. Twelve-thousand dollars later, she had more things for her closet, her husband's closet, her lover's closet, and new toys for the children. By the time she got home, she collapsed into her settee with aching feet and a sore back.

"The master is calling, madame," another of the staff said, holding a silver platter with a cordless receiver on it. She rolled her eyes. Indra was kind to her, but so over the top with irrational things and such a penny-pincher with others that it made her twitch sometimes.

"Thank you, Sherie," she said, then picked up the phone. "My most humble husband calls. To what do I owe the pleasure? – – God, Indra, it was just therapy. You're going to love the things I got for you. – – No. Jessica Viejo was picking on Q. – – Well, it was shop or stab her with my shrimp fork. – – That was my thinking. See? We agree. Will you be back soon? – – No, I'm fine. Farah misses you. – – She'll like that. – – Ok. – – No, no more therapy. – – Yes, I understand I have an actual therapist. – – Yeah. I'll tell them. – – Bye."

Bella hung up the phone and set it back on the silver platter. The maid that brought it in bobbed a curtsey and left. Bella *was* the fairy tale. Married to a tribe prince from a middle eastern country that controlled a lot of oil. They had a home in Dubai, one in London, Germany, Washington, New York, and three vacation homes in the tropics. Her father married her to Indra Amad for the oil money. The man was handsome enough, gave her whatever she wanted, and was decent enough in bed – when he was around. He spent most of his time in Dubai. Bella and her children spent most of their time in London. She'd been visiting her parents when the news broke of Quinn's nuptials.

Whatever Quinn was playing at, he was winning a good game. As much as Bella hated to admit it, she was kind of jealous of her little brother. She sighed, glanced at the small touchpad near the side table and whined. Instead, she pulled out her cell phone and hit a button.

"Yes, ma'am," a male voice answered, coming from the touchpad rather than her phone.

"Run me a bath," she said without moving. Her bathroom was ten feet away. "With you in it."

"Of course, ma'am."

That was it. The page ended. Twenty minutes later, she sat in a hot, bubble-filled bath with a gloriously well-built man lavishing her neck in kisses while his strong hands massaged the tension from her shoulders.

"Why so tense?" he murmured against her damp skin. She leaned to the side, giving him access to her.

"My brother's gay," she grumped. He chortled through his nose against her neck. "Seriously. He's engaged to his roommate. Mom just blasted it all out on Facebook yesterday."

"Wow," he smiled, still kissing her neck, now gently massaging her breasts to make her moan. "Good for him."

Bella let her agitation go, leaning back against her lover's chest so he could give her pleasure instead of thinking about her stupid brother and his practically perfect life – the life *she* couldn't afford.

#

Gage Lang lay sprawled across a padded lounge chair, soaking in what little sunlight hit Seattle like a lizard beneath a heat lamp set on a timer. The entire house was buzzing with news after his parents return from D.C. He'd languished in the blessed *silence* of the monolithic house his parents lived in. Something was *always* happening. People came and went either for business or pleasure – sometimes both. Most of the time Gage did his best to hide away in his room, feigning a need to study rather than socialize. It usually worked. When it didn't, Gage shuffled through his parents' shenanigans, as high as a kite on cocaine to curb the temptation to impale himself on a nine iron.

His phone buzzed on the glass table beside him. He ignored it until it buzzed four more times. Someone was being insistent. When he picked it up, he realized who that someone was and groaned.

From: WILLOW THE FREAK

|Did u hear?

From: WILLOW THE FREAK

|Don't ignore me.

From: WILLOW THE FREAK

|Gage!

From: WILLOW THE FREAK

|GAGE!

It was the all-caps text of his name that did it. His sister was a beast on the best of days. Bella wasn't so bad, but Willow was like the Creature from the Black Lagoon. She lived in Beverly Hills – thank God. But with all the news bubbling around Quinn and his coming nuptials, it was just a matter of time before Willow showed up. If nothing else, she needed to be there to 'comfort' Racine Fier. The two were inseparable despite not living in the same state. Just based on Willow's Instagram account, the two found ways around the distance.

Gage did not feel the need to reply via text, tapping his bluetooth so he could *call* rather than force his fingers to move more than necessary. Text did not convey everything in language, anyway. It stripped away the emotive part of a language. Well, maybe not from Willow but she had a way of making everything sound like a screech.

"What?" Gage said when his sister finally answered the phone. "Willow, I live here still, of course I've heard. – – Why do *you* care? – – Because the letter of the agreement isn't based on the who, just the timing. – – Yes, I've read it. Have you? – – Will, get to the point, I'm baking and you're ruining my buzz. – – God, why do you do this to me? – – Whatever. – – No, I will not play messenger to Racine. She has a phone. Screech at her on your own. – – I said, no, Will. Fly up here and talk to her yourself."

Gage ended the call after that, sighing heavily when his phone buzzed; again. He let it buzz once more before reading the new texts.

From: WILLOW THE FREAK

|DO NOT IGNORE ME! I WILL TELL MOM AND DAD!

From: RACINE FIER

|Don't ignore her, twat. This is important. Dinner. Tomorrow. Be there.

"For fuck's sake..." Gage groaned just as the

clouds rolled back over the sun, as if God himself was sending a portent of things to come.

56

clouds rolled back over the sun, as if God himself was sending a portent of things to come.

06

Angel stared at the tiny mutt that Rachel loved so much. He kept a good five foot distance from it, watching as it growled at him anytime he so much as scratched his nose. He'd spent the night with Rachel plenty of times, but the dog was usually locked up for his benefit. It was the only animal on the entire planet that he hated with the fire of a thousand suns.

"Juju! Come!" Rachel called. The beast trotted away, tail wagging like it was not just threatening to launch itself at Angel's throat. He listened to Rachel lock the animal away, remaining as still as possible until Rachel came back out to the living room. "Staying in or going out tonight?"

"Yes?" Angel replied. "Is that an option?"

Rachel laughed at him. He sighed, shuffling to her couch before dropping onto it heavily enough to make the spring bounce. Rachel joined him, pulling him against her shoulder.

"I'm sorry, baby. If it's such a hassle why are you doing it?" Rachel asked.

"Quinn," Angel answered without thought or hesitation. "God, Rae if you saw him that night you'd be marrying him too. It was like watching someone beat on a three-legged, blind puppy."

"Ouch. That bad?"

Angel nodded, sitting up so he could face Rachel. "Your dog and I have a better relationship than Quinn has with his parents. His *adopted* parents. I didn't even know he *was* adopted! Who hides shit like that? Why? Well, let me tell you why – because they're rich, judgmental, assholes, that's why. I just...people like them only exist in movies, Rachel."

"Movies gotta get their ideas from something, right?" Rachel offered. Angel just Kermit-stared at her in response. She giggled. He loved when she giggled. He loved how *comfortable* he felt with her. Dog not withstanding, Rachel's place was warm and inviting, with furniture pilfered from thrift stores, or yard sales, and greenery all over the place. Things between Angel and Quinn felt so *weird* right now that being home put a knot in his stomach. Yes, he agreed to whatever crazy arrangement the Langs demanded but, at the same time, he felt that if he *didn't* agree to it Quinn was not going to make it to see his thirtieth birthday and that scared him more than the prospect of fake marrying him, or any oddness that sprouted between them.

"What did your mom say?" Rachel asked. Angel groaned. "Uh oh."

Rachel spent as much time with Angel's fabulously large family as Quinn did. They asked every time when he was going to propose or when Rachel was going to make him buy that ring. Most of the time it was in jest but, every now and then Angel could hear the seriousness in their ribbing. Now, with Quinn...

"She asked me why I didn't tell her I was gay sooner and if you were going to carry our babies," Angel stated in flat tones. Rachel blinked at him. "Yeah, I know."

"Wow," Rachel breathed. "That's... either the most supportive thing a parent could say or the most presumptuous. What if you two don't want kids?"

"I don't think that thought has ever crossed her mind. Ever. I'm one of *seven*, Rachel. It's just expected. And I do, maybe. Not *now* but, maybe someday, you know?"

Rachel merely nodded. Angel knew why and simply pulled her into his arms.

"Angel?"

"Yeah?" he replied, still holding her.

"Has Quinn ever kissed a guy?"

\#

"No. No! Dammit!" Quinn growled. Angel laughed, shoving his friend in the shoulder while Rachel chopped up fresh veggies from the farmer's market in their kitchen. Quinn could hear the rhythmic chopping motions against their butcher block. It was a gigantic thing that Quinn bought as a Christmas gift for Angel since the man was so crunchy granola he may as well eat bark. It was not entirely unusual for Rachel to stop by after, or even stay the night. Farmer's market was their thing. Video games was Quinn's thing. Video games that he was currently sucking at.

"You cheated," Quinn complained. Angel laughed harder, shaking his head. It was adorable. It would be *more* adorable if Rachel were not around. Her presence bothered Quinn when, normally, it wouldn't.

"You're just saying that because my turtle knocked you off your cart," Angel said. He tossed his hair back, cracked his neck and reset the game for another round.

"Just throw banana peels or oil. You'll gain advantage faster that way," Rachel said as she came to join the boys in the living room, planting herself on the edge of the couch until Angel moved to make room for her. Quinn merely gave her a suspicious look and scooted as well so he wouldn't be *that* close to Angel.

"How would you know?" Quinn said, settling into a more comfortable position that didn't put his elbow right into Angel's ribs or vice versa.

"I play too, you know," Rachel chuckled. She offered the plate of fresh veggies to the boys. Angel took one. Quinn declined on principle.

He didn't like that Rachel played video games. It was entirely absurd to think that way, but Quinn was also an entirely absurd individual. Video games was *his* thing. Farmer's markets were *Rachel's* thing. She needed to get that straight. Which, of course sounded stupid even in Quinn's overactive mind.

"Oh, the purple cart is fun!" Rachel continued. "Do I get to play winner?"

"Sure," Angel answered right as Quinn said "No."

Quinn followed his response up with a frustrated glower in Angel's direction. He caught the look Angel shared with Rachel too and huffed away from the couch before the race could start.

"Hey," Angel said, following shortly thereafter. "I thought we were gonna play? What's wrong with you?"

"Nothing, just forget it. Play with *Rachel*," Quinn said then kicked himself when he realized how much sass he put into her name. There was nothing wrong with Rachel. She was nice, and pretty for a girl. She made good baked ziti, and had a tiny little Chihuahua that licked Quinn's fingers anytime he saw her. He didn't know the dog's name, but she was cute. Angel hated her though so Quinn never offered to have the dog come when Rachel did. But something about today just rubbed Quinn in all the wrong ways.

"Q? Come on, man. We're on a streak," Angel said with a gesture out to the living room where Rachel played while the boys talked. Quinn's ire rose. Angel saw it and glanced out to the living room then shut the door. "Is it Rachel?"

"No," Quinn snipped then sighed. "I dunno. Maybe. I just... games are *our* thing, Angel. Not hers."

"Quinn Lang, are you *jealous*?" Angel laughed.

"This is why I don't talk to you," Quinn deadpanned. Angel laughed harder. "Get out. Just... go. I'll putz around in here or something."

"And do what? Watch porn while we hang out? That's stupid," Angel chortled while glancing around Quinn's room. It had his workstation on a wall that didn't get any light from the window.

The bed sat beneath that and there was a TV mounted to the wall across from it. It was the workstation that drew all attention. The thing was massive, with screens all over, and a chair that tilted backwards so Quinn could work upside down if he wanted. The desk moved too, rising up and down, even tilting a little to follow the chair. Quinn liked pretending he was in a plane when he did that. Or a space ship. He was the most immature twenty-nine-year-old on the planet.

"Quinn, is this about the engagement?" Angel said when Quinn lost himself in his work habits and creature comforts. Instead of answering, he felt his face turn red and his ears burn. "Quinn?"

"Maybe, ok? Maybe, I dunno. This is all really weird and really stupid and..."

"Quinn, we're not in a real relationship," Angel pointed out.

"I know that, ok? I know."

Angel blinked at him as things began to click in place in ways that Quinn could practically see. Quinn's ears burned hotter as a result.

"Do you want it to be?" Angel finally said. Quinn stayed silent, feeling his gut roil, but shook his head anyway. "Quinn?"

Silence.

"Whatever. We said we weren't going to let

things get weird. You just made it weird. I'm going to take Rachel home. I'll let you know if I stay or not."

Quinn let Angel go without saying anything while trying not to cry over how things were already changing – and falling apart.

#

Angel stayed at Rachel's place clear through the following Saturday when Quinn called to apologize for being a jealous dick. Even then, it took another few days for things to feel normal again.

"God, those new people downstairs run around like fucking rhinos on speed," Angel said as he came out of the bathroom into the living room that Wednesday. He broke weekly tradition with Rachel for Quinn's sake.

"No shit," Quinn said, glancing over his shoulder to catch sight of Angel in thin pajama bottoms, skin still glistening from the shower. Logically, he knew it wasn't anything he hadn't seen before. He'd lived with the man for six years, with only *one* bathroom between them. They may not be high maintenance men, but sometimes nature called while the shower trickled, and Angel forbade pissing in the composting machine. However, the illogical, emotional part of Quinn delighting in the thought of marrying his long-time crush suddenly made his heart race and his pants tent a little at the sight of Angel's bare chest.

"What's wrong with you? Your ears are turning red."

Quinn curled his fingers tightly around the controller in his hands so as not to immediately throw them over his ears. "N–nothing. Tired, I guess."

"Since when do your ears turn red from being tired?" Angel asked, moving around to the front of the couch. Quinn stopped breathing. "I'm not even going to ask."

He didn't need to. Quinn knew to what Angel was referring because it literally *stood out* in a very embarrassing, very awkward way.

"Take care of it in the bathroom, dude," Angel continued, walking back around the couch toward his room. Quinn silently wished for all clothing to fall into a black hole and never return. Angel looked *good* without a shirt. He just plain looked *good.*

"Angel, I'm gay," Quinn blurted, feeling the heat rise in his face even more.

Silence.

Quinn looked at his lap, willing the hard–on in his pants to go away while making it worse at the same time. Angel moved into a position that blocked the light from the TV, making Quinn freeze and his brain turn off. His dick was in control now.

"Quinn," Angel began in a tone that suggested he was either going to be furious or laugh his ass off. "Do you have a chubby in your pants because of *me*?"

Quinn's stomach sank. He *wanted* the lie, *wanted* to believe they were a real couple and that his racing heart was not just mild psychosis. Truth was, he'd never been with a guy before. He daydreamed about it, watched plenty of porn, but had been crushing on Angel since he realized he liked men and never pursued anyone else.

"Quinn?"

"What?" Quinn finally sighed, daring to look up at Angel's stunning face. "Yes, alright, I *like* the way you look. Yes, I *like* you. I have for a while. But I didn't want to make things weird, so I never said anything. No one knows. I talk to maybe five people and none of them are interested in my messed-up *lack* of sex life. And you've got Rachel so..."

Silence.

Quinn waited, palms growing sweaty as the silence stretched on. "Are... you going to say something?"

"You've never had a steady girlfriend — or, boyfriend, as it were — because you've had a crush on *me* this whole time?" Angel asked.

"I'm trying really hard to not make this worse than it already is, Angel," Quinn sighed.

"Failing. Big time." Quinn threw a glower at Angel, surprised to find a smirk on the other man's face. Quinn's torment amused him. "Does *anyone* know?"

"No. Well, I guess they do *now* but, no," Quinn grumbled, hands still desperately trying to shove his hard-on back down. It wasn't working. Angel noticed.

"I'm going to bed," Angel laughed. "Lock the door to the bathroom, please. I don't want to walk in on you."

Quinn just groaned and shoved his way past Angel to the bathroom. He could hear Angel chuckling, feel his heart breaking as a result, and just slid down the length of the door to fist his hair in his hands. This was *exactly* what he was afraid of, and *exactly* the kind of thing that would absolutely ruin the relationship he had with his best friend.

It was the thing that made Quinn just want to drown himself in the toilet; the thing that had him avoiding Angel at all costs for the next few weeks.

07

By the end of June, things had gone from awkward, to weird, to oddly uncomfortable between Angel and Quinn. Angel tried to be more understanding of the situation but it was hard – especially when he checked the day's mail. Angel looked down at the announcement in his hand with an arched brow. It was a soft cream color on paper that probably killed an entire tree to produce, stamped with real gold fillagree. It read, 'We are delighted to announce the engagement of our son, Quinn Anthony Lang to his partner, Angel Jesus Rivera.' Beneath that, it detailed the arrangements to celebrate and marry in the Lang family values – – in *Italy*.

"Quinn..." Angel said, still looking at the card in his hand. Quinn did not respond. Angel's eyes rolled up to glower at Quinn's room. He could see the light from Quinn's workstation washing out the room in a hazy, ghostly blue and hear the keys clicking. "Quinn!"

Silence.

Angel grumbled as he walked into Quinn's room and ripped the headphones off his roommate's head. Metallica pumped out of them at a volume that could deafen an elephant.

"Hey! I'm working!" Quinn complained. Angel shoved the announcement card in his face.

"Italy?" Angel inquired. Quinn sagged. "*Italy, Quinn?*"

Quinn groaned, taking the announcement card. To his benefit, he looked like he might be sick.

The entire 'event' would take place at some castle in Italy. Angel had never heard of anything so absurd. No, he had; in the romance movies he and Rachel watched people got married in big, fancy, *expensive* places. There was no way to keep any of this a secret now.

Originally, Leti kept things mostly under wraps from everyone except Angel's *tia* and his mom, who called to yell at him for not telling her he was gay *or* in love with Quinn — which he wasn't, no matter how much Quinn might want it. By the end of that week, most of Angel's family knew something was up. The rest of the time was spent trying to *not* be weird around the roommate – who was, in fact, gay *and* in love with him – with little success. Now Italy. From an announcement he was *positive* went to his parents and extended family. He didn't have that kind of time off from work or that many clothes, either. No one did. Then, Quinn's phone rang.

"God," Quinn groaned. He took a deep breath and hit the speaker button, putting on a smile so fake, Angel looked around to make sure he was still in the right room. "Hey, Bells."

"Hey, Q!" a woman said, her voice dripping with fake honey. "Get the announcements yet? Aren't they just too chic? Is your boy around? I have ideas..."

The woman kept droning on without letting Quinn *or* Angel speak. A coordinator had already been hired, the rooms were being prepped. They could only find part of Angel's family for the announcements and, oh, did they all have green cards or passports or whatever Hispanics used? Angel nearly crushed the phone. Instead, he walked out of the room.

"Fifty million, fifty million, fifty million..." he repeated over and over. He was so angry, it was nearly enough to induce a seizure. So, he went to his room to take slow, deep breaths to calm down. When Quinn knocked on his door, he cracked a single eye open to look at the other man.

"Sorry," Quinn said, leaning against the door frame. Angel opened his other eye. "I told you they sucked."

"They're really flying us out to Italy?" Angel asked. Quinn nodded sadly. Anyone else would be thrilled at the prospect of visiting Italy in such a lavish fashion. Quinn seemed defeated by it. Angel fell somewhere in between. The furthest he'd been out of the country was Canada for work, and Mexico for really large, really loud family reunions every five years. Italy was rather enticing, no matter the reason.

Two weeks later, Quinn and Angel sat on a flight from Reagan International to Galileo Galilei Airport on a private charter to Tuscany where an *entire castle* had been rented for three weeks' worth of festivities. Angel's parents declined the invitation, unable to get the time off work. Leti and Rachel accepted instead. Angel brought his work with him because three weeks' vacation was *not* possible for the working class. Rachel brought hers too, both of them chatting on the flight.

Quinn didn't say a word throughout the entire plane ride, and kept biting his fingers as they were taken to the venue by a private driver. They'd gone shopping for new clothes, new shoes, and a fake engagement ring with Leti and Rachel tagging along to help or buy their own things. Appearances were very important to the Langs.

"So, why can't I talk about wildlife preservation?" Angel asked, looking at a list of things to avoid as they drove through the breathtaking country.

"My dad has a room full of stuffed heads because hunting is a man's sport and man should always show the creatures of the earth who the apex predator is," Quinn said, as if reciting that from memory. Angel blinked. "He's not going to tolerate anyone trying to tell him *not* to shoot the last white rhino on Earth. Or that straws hurt sea turtles."

"But they do," Angel argued. Quinn threw a frustrated glance at him, then turned his attention back out the window. "You're kinda freaking me out right now with how much you're freaking out. It's not like we're moving in with them. We're getting fake married – in *Italy*, I might add – and then going home."

"Dammit, Angel, you know you just cursed us?" Quinn growled while marking himself with the sign of the cross, despite the fact Quinn was atheist.

Angel just shook his head, jaw going slack when they finally drove up to the wrought-iron gate around the property. Vineyards covered every inch of the surrounding grounds. Mountains could be seen in the distance, and the 'venue' was actually a castle with four other smaller villas on the surrounding acreage.

"Holy fuck..." Angel breathed. Quinn did not seem impressed.

"Don't let my siblings corner you alone. They're brutal. And dear God, don't let my dad corner you either."

Angel opted to stay quiet after that. He surveyed everything with a wistful smile as he exited the car. Staff came to take their belongings and escort them into the castle. A second car followed with Rachel and Leti.

"Angel, c'mon," Quinn said, drawing Angel's attention. He'd stopped to admire the scenery, something he was positive no one in the Lang family – or any of their insane number of guests – had ever done. To them, it was just leaves and bricks. To Angel, it was a magical fairy tale.

"It's nice here," Angel commented as he caught up.

"I hate it here," Quinn replied before nearly colliding with three screaming kids barreling around the limestone entryway of the castle.

"STOP RUNNING IN THE CASTLE!"

"Bella," Quinn explained. "Those are her kids."

"Quinn!" the woman said, coming around the corner on three-inch wedge sandals and skin-tight leather pants like a runway model on Ru Paul's Drag Race. Much like Mr. and Mrs. Lang had done, she hugged Quinn with all the affection of a slow-moving glacier. The act was practiced, not heartfelt. "Is this him?"

"Who?" Quinn said. Angel cringed. "Oh! Oh, yeah! Angel, this is Bella. Bells, Angel."

"Well, aren't you a catch," Bella said, looking Angel up and down like meat. "Good job, Q."

Quinn visibly sagged.

"I've got you guys all set up in the bridal suite. Mom's got lunch scheduled for— GODDAMMIT, I SAID STOP RUNNING!"

And that was the end of their conversation with Bella. Angel watched her stomp off after her children. There was noise all around, ranging from music to the beeps and squeaks of a video game. At the bottom of a winding set of stairs was a girl of roughly ten with a Switch in her hands and headphones on her head. She glanced up at them once, waved, then went back to her game without expecting a response. Quinn didn't notice.

"C'mon, let's just go upstairs until lunch," Quinn huffed, following a staff member to the bridal suite. Angel glanced down at the girl as they passed her, offering a smile that lit up her eyes when she caught sight of it. Angel wanted to ask who she was, but stopped when they reached the suite in question. It was the size of their entire apartment.

"Jesus, Q..." Angel breathed out. Quinn said nothing, checking out the bathroom. The bed was some sort of monstrous California King with real silk and goose down. Angel cringed. He hated using animal products as decor. "So, is there protocol for lunch or...?"

"Protocol. We'll eat outside in an hour. Bella sent the itinerary," Quinn sighed. "There's a granola bar in my backpack if you're hungry now."

"You're still freaking out, aren't you?" Angel asked. Quinn hung his head, looking miserable.

"What am I going to do when we need to *show* that we're madly in love, Angel? I managed at dinner with my parents because I chalked it up to being caught off guard. Now they're expecting to see us together all the time and they'll be *watching*. There's no way we're going to make it through *three weeks* without them noticing something is off!"

Angel arched a brow at Quinn. The outburst explained why his friend was so nervous since leaving the US. Or why he wanted to go run and hide in their room as soon as they arrived. Or why he picked at his fingers and bit his nails while standing there overthinking the entire process. He knew there was more to it than just immediate nerves, things neither man spoke of out of a need to maintain the status quo. However, the status quo changed the second Quinn's parents set foot in their lives.

So Angel stood up and gently took Quinn's hand from his mouth, giving it a little squeeze that made the other man freeze.

"Breathe, Quinn," Angel directed. "Inhale through your nose, exhale through your mouth."

"Angel..." Quinn whined. It was a practiced routine with them. Quinn was always wound tight as a copper coil.

"Quinn, breathe," Angel said with a little more force. Angel demonstrated, watching Quinn follow his lead until the man's muscles relaxed. He still wore a pout of worry on his face and held tight to Angel's hand, but it was progress. "Think of it like a game. Like, a LARP session."

"LARPing is different," Quinn groaned. They hadn't done live action role-play in a while, but it was something they took part in often during college. Their group even still met twice a year for a full weekend of costumed nerdery.

"Not really. We're playing a character. Sure, it's a not four-hundred-year-old vampire or a band of elven thieves, but it's generally the same. There are relationships and plots in our LARPing games, just like this game. We hit Level 1 the night you told me you were gay. I'll group hand holding into Level 1. And," Angel said looking at his hand laced with Quinn's. "Achievement unlocked."

Quinn snorted.

"We hug all the time, and wrestle, right? Doing that here is no different," Angel said, pulling Quinn into a hug. The man melted, burying his face into Angel's collarbone. "Level 2 achieved."

"I hate that you're using game terms for this."

"Only because you understand it better," Angel laughed. "The hardest part for you is going to be Level 3, I think."

"It won't be for you?" Quinn asked, looking up at Angel, still in his embrace. Angel smirked, eyebrow arched.

"Quinn, I'm getting fifty *million* dollars. I'll kiss a crocodile for that money."

"That doesn't make me feel better, but good to know where your standards–"

Angel silenced Quinn's thoughts by giving him a chaste kiss. Nothing major, but enough to rob the poor gaming troll of breath and tighten his muscles again. Quinn even kept his eyes closed when Angel pulled away.

"Ok, you've gotta work on that part, Q. Breathe, and we'll try Level 3 again in a minute." Quinn just groaned and threw himself face-first onto the bed. Angel stared down at him, then sat beside Quinn. "You're going to keep freaking out, aren't you?"

"I can't believe you're not!" Quinn whined as he flipped himself over. "Why aren't you!"

"Because it doesn't do any good, Quinn," Angel sighed. "We're already here. It doesn't change what we have to do. It won't change what your family already thinks of me *or* you. They treat you like shit and you let them. You're worried because you're afraid of what they'll think, for reasons I cannot fathom."

He let that sink in a little before huffing out a little sigh, then smacked Quinn's arm. "So, come on. We need to get Level 3 nailed down before dinner, for sure, or they *will* say something."

"You suck," Quinn grumbled.

"That's, like, at least Level 5, dude and *you'll* be the one sucking, not me," Angel smirked. Quinn glowered at him.

#

"Mackenzie, get off that machine," Elliott Lang sighed. He walked past his daughter to the bartender in the family suite and had the man pour him a glass of a bourbon. Mackenzie watched him. "Don't you want to go outside? There's horses. And a maze."

Mackenzie shrugged her shoulders, then watched her mother enter the room. Elliott, turned back toward the bartender.

"Elliott, it's barely past noon," Paige Lang sighed.

"It's one drink," Elliott said, downing what was in his tumbler. He didn't say anything else, walking out with a little pat to Mackenzie's head. The castle Bella's planner found was luxurious with the full amenities of a resort and then some. Elliott found his way to the *other* bar for another drink. He was three down before anyone else came into the bar. A woman. Elliott's interest was immediately piqued.

He didn't recognize her, a cute Hispanic young woman. Probably the groom's family. Rumor had it none of them wanted to come. Some weird falling out. Elliott didn't care. The chick had a nice ass.

"You from... uhm... the groom's family?" he asked. He couldn't remember the guy's name. It didn't matter, anyway.

"Angel," she said as she nodded. "Yeah, he's my brother."

"Oh yeah? So why aren't the rest of your family here? Don't approve of him being gay?"

Elliott smirked. The young woman arched a brow, then turned to face him with a sweet smile.

"No, they don't like white people," she said, accepting her drink before walking away.

Leti giggled as she left the bar. The castle was *gorgeous*. Her parents so desperately wanted to come, but time off work was not a concept the Langs seemed to understand. She went out to the back patio, where Rachel sat at a table. She was Angel's work wife. It was cute. She'd make a good actual wife for Angel. Everyone said so. It made Leti wonder what would happen now that Angel was 'marrying' Quinn. There had to be more to it than just money.

"Hey," Leti said, sitting down beside the other woman. "So, anyone hit on you yet?"

"Uhm... the Egyptian guy?" Rachel said. Leti nodded. Same guy. "Can you believe all this?"

"Nope," Leti said, sipping her drink happily. "So, you and Angel?"

"What? No! He's with Quinn!"

"Rachel, he told me the story. Angel can't keep things from me," Leti replied. Rachel flushed.

"It's not serious..."

"Jealous?" Leti pressed. The other woman whipped her head around so fast her earrings clacked against her neck.

"God, no!" Rachel giggled. "Honestly, I've been wondering which one of us would finally win. Money definitely beats out a good lay."

Leti giggled again. She'd made the same observation of her brother. He didn't have interest in anyone else because he was perfectly content to remain within the walls of his perfect little world. This was a big step outside of that box, though Leti imagined the same was true for Quinn.

The devils appeared shortly thereafter, holding hands like the couple they were meant to be. Hugs and kisses went around before they sat back down to overlook the mountain paths behind the castle.

"This place is gorgeous," Rachel breathed as another glass of wine was brought to her. "Service is nice, too. Very bougie, Q."

"Shut up," Quinn groaned. Everyone but Quinn laughed.

"Ok, we're here to help. What can we do?" Leti asked.

"Nothing," Quinn said. "Please. Don't even offer. Someone *will* get offended."

Leti looked at Angel, who shook his head. She looked at Rachel next, who shrugged. Leti scrunched her face up and looked at Quinn until the man felt her growing ire and looked up at her.

"What?" he dared.

"We're here to help *you,* asshole. You're grumping around like you *don't* want to get married. Smile a little, yeah? You're marrying *my* brother. He's a catch. Be grateful."

Rachel choked on her wine, making Leti smirk. Quinn just threw a glare at Rachel.

"Have you kissed him yet, at least?" Leti whispered. Quinn glared at Leti next. Leti glowered back. "Quinn! You're getting *married.* They think you've fucked him already! Act like it!"

"Ok, knock it off. That isn't helping," Angel said, putting a hand on Quinn's bouncing knee. "We're working on it."

"Work faster, they're coming," Rachel muttered, then took a drink from her glass. The woman with the screaming kids, and two people that Leti could only guess were Quinn's parents based on their age, came to join them with fake smiles plastered to their fake faces.

"There they are!" Mrs. Lang practically sang, stooping to give Quinn a weak hug. She mirrored the act on Angel. "We've been looking all over for you! Did you get your engagement outfits? I had Sonora press them earlier."

"Engagement outfits?" Quinn asked.

"Yeah, mom got new outfits for you guys for tomorrow's engagement party. She wants to make sure they fit," the younger woman said. She wore pants that looked like they might suffocate her. Leti tried not to sneer.

"Mom," Quinn whined.

"Stop slouching, Quinn," the woman replied, rather than listen to Quinn's complaints. She pushed on the spot between Quinn's shoulder blades to make him sit straight as she continued to admonish him. "Honestly, how did you even get a *boyfriend* with all your bad habits? God, not even *Racine* would want what you have."

Quinn turned red. Angel did too, for different reasons, but Leti kicked her brother's foot to stop him from letting his temper fly.

"She doesn't have to," Angel smiled. "I want him just the way he is."

Leti watched her brother kiss Quinn's hand and smile at him like Quinn meant the absolute world to him. Quinn smirked back, flushing to the roots of his hair. It was adorable even if it was fake. Well, mostly fake. Leti knew how much Quinn meant to Angel. The guy came to every holiday and family gathering because he *was* family to Angel. That was enough for Leti.

"Of course you do," Mrs. Lang dismissed. "We have lunch planned in an hour and then you two can try on your outfits before we go to the spring for photos–"

"Mom," Quinn cut in. "Can we just... get a

day to breathe? We'll try the outfits on later, ok?"

"Quinn, this is important to your mother," Mr. Lang said. "You can take a few minutes to try on a suit."

"Sure," Rachel said, coming to the rescue before *Leti* said something. "Leti and I can make sure they tie their ties right and take a bottle of wine to go. We'll see you at lunch?"

"Sounds perfect," the younger woman intoned. "Mom, the cake?"

"Right," Mrs. Lang said. "Quinn, make sure you wear the Spanx. I don't want your beer belly showing in the picture."

Leti nearly said something that time, biting her tongue because Angel kicked *her* foot. She took in a breath and held it until the three idiots were gone before releasing it while looking at Quinn. "Holy fuck, are they always like this?"

"Yes," Quinn groaned.

The Langs, Leti decided, were assholes.

08

Angel stared at a set of rolling racks positively stuffed with clothing bags. Each bag had two outfits – one for himself and one for Quinn. Angel had to count twice to be sure he got the number right. There were twenty-two different bags. Well, twenty-one. One had been pulled out when Angel and Quinn arrived in the room try everything on and prep for their *first* photoshoot.

"Angel," Quinn pleaded as the tailor quite literally stuffed him into something that looked like a sausage compactor, but with more torture. Angel even went so far as to wince on his friend's behalf. Quinn wasn't *that* fluffy. He didn't work out as much as Angel did, but he certainly didn't require the contraption he was being forced to wear, either.

"Uhm... does he have to wear that?" Angel interrupted. The woman paused and looked at Angel, blinking benignly, as if she did not understand him. Sonora was her name. Angel arched his brow at her, then repeated the question in Spanish.

"The lady of the house requested that he wear it to make him look more thin," the woman replied in Spanish.

"The lady of the house isn't the one wearing it. Take it off. Please." Angel said, then handed the woman forty dollars to just leave them in peace. She shrugged, pocketed her money, and left the room.

"Help."

Angel chuckled. He went straight to Quinn, helping the man out of the stupid contraption Sonora was trying to paste on him. Once the last hook came off, Quinn finally let out a sigh of relief. Red marks marred his sides and belly.

"Sorry," Angel said.

"You weren't stuffing me in that thing," Quinn replied, leaning over his knees.

They'd stayed holed up in their room after lunch practicing Level 3, until both of them finally decreed it was, at the very least, passable. Angel was tired, a little cranky, and didn't get nearly enough to eat for breakfast before they left for the airport.

"I've seen corsets that aren't as torturous as whatever that thing is," Angel quipped. "You ok?"

"I can breathe. It's a start," he said then frowned, turning his head to face Angel, hands still on knees. "Corsets?"

"Rachel has a few of them. She looks damn good in them too."

"Why-"

"Ren Fair, Quinn. That place I can never get you to go to because – and I will quote – it's too hot and/or cold to wear garb and it isn't right to go to one in jeans and flannel."

"I do not say that," Quinn retorted, standing sharply, then faltering enough that Angel caught him. "Ugh... head rush."

"Smile, lovebirds!" Bella said. Her voice startled them both, making them whirl on the woman who snapped a photo right when they faced her, both of them looking like terrified deer. At least, that's how Angel felt.

"Bella, what are you doing!" Quinn growled.

"Candids. Makes for a better photo collage if there's some candids in it to go with all the staged ones. What happened to your stomach, Q? You guys doing something kinky?"

"Funny," Quinn glowered. "No. Sonora tried

to stuff me into some sort of torture device to make my stomach flatter."

Bella looked at her brother's exposed torso, then at Angel with a deadpan look. "I mean it's ok... could be better."

"It's *fine*," Angel emphasized, wishing everyone would stop picking on Quinn for longer than ten minutes at a time.

"Oh yeah, I mean sure, if that's what you like," Bella shrugged then looked at Angel and shrank a little. "Which ... you obviously do, so bonus. More pics?"

"Seriously, Bella, just go so we can get dressed for mom's dumb dinner," Quinn sighed. She rolled her eyes, but let them be.

Dinner was full of pomp and circumstance that served no purpose other than to parade the wealth and hobnob with the snobs. Angel hated every second of it. He stayed close to Leti and Rachel, even when Quinn was dragged away by his mother or father and berated for this or that. They found a reason to tear him down about *everything* from the way he stood to the way he held a fork.

"Poor Quinn," Rachel commented during one of the berating sessions. "Go save him or something. Or I'll go save him. Someone go save him. This is painful to watch."

"I'll go," Angel said, absently raising one of

Rachel's hands to his lips for a kiss as he got to his feet. He gave Leti's knee a squeeze then steeled himself as if readying for battle.

"... this is all going to work, champ, but this is important," Mr. Lang was saying. What could be so important as to make Quinn slouch and pout, Angel could only imagine.

"Hey, mind if I cut in? Music just started," Angel said. Quinn looked more terrified of what Angel was implying than of his father's harsh words.

"Oh, uh, yeah, go ahead," Mr. Lang said with a fake smile as if Angel truly needed the man's permission to dance with his fiancé – fake or otherwise.

Angel managed to grin back, taking Quinn's hand in his to lead him toward where people were dancing.

"What are you doing?" Quinn asked.

"Saving your ass," Angel replied dryly.

"Angel, I can't dance!" Quinn hissed.

"Pretend," Angel said, pulling him into a dancing embrace, only to have Quinn smash his toe. "Ow. Quinn..."

"I'm sorry! I'm.. I told you I can't dance," he hissed. Angel put on a smile as fake as the ones the Langs gave and slowly moved in a circle.

"Just keep your feet in between mine

and move with me, ok?" Angel replied through clenched teeth against Quinn's ear. Bella snapped a picture in that moment, making it appear as if the two were cuddling close. "Ignore her."

"Can't. She just blinded me. You were looking the other way," Quinn replied. "God, can we just go back to the room?"

"Yeah... after this," Angel agreed. "Otherwise I might stab someone."

#

Gage Lang let a stream of smoke rise up into the night sky. More and more people filtered into the castle's massive dining hall, all of them friends of his parents. The handful of people his own age were children of those friends, none of which Gage cared to associate with. Willow and Racine had already had a bitch fest about Quinn's beau, cursing the man in at least three languages. Gage understood them all. They all had their specialties – well, maybe not Willow.

Elliott got the mad medical skills, digging into people's brains like Bella's kids dug into Jello. Bella was business savvy like their mom, already racking up millions on her own doing international real estate. Quinn was the coolest so far, programming video games that sold out across the globe. Gage was still finding his place, but he had a good ear for languages, picking them up like tattoos – they simply branded themselves onto his mind. He remembered everything, too. His high school counselor once said it was an eidetic memory. Gage said it was bullshit. Still, he landed himself at Stanford on a full ride in the linguistics department. He thought about going to Japan or Croatia or even Columbia, where he was born. But all of that required work, so he hadn't bothered with it yet.

Then there was Willow.

The copper-goddess of cosmetics wandered over with her black hair falling down to the point just above her perfectly sculpted ass. And it *was* sculpted. Nothing that round happened in nature. Out of habit and instinct, Gage reached for the white baggie in his pocket and took a quick sniff of coke. He would need it to deal with his stupid sister.

"Racine was looking for you," Willow purred into his ear, making him shiver. He hated when she did that. It was weird. *She* was weird.

"Why?" Gage asked, blowing out another stream of smoke towards the stars above him.

"Mom was too, loser," Willow continued, running her hands along his shoulders and neck. He shrugged her off.

"Stop, Will. Don't be weird, ok?"

"Aww, baby boy, that's not what you told

me before," she cackled. Gage threw her a flat glare.

Get **one** *hard-on after seeing your sister naked and she never lets it* go... he thought, doing his best to let her words roll off his back. He'd been fourteen, for Christ's sake. Any fourteen-year-old would have gotten a hard-on – even Quinn!

"Racie wants to know why the guy's still breathing, Gage," Willow finally said, digging her nails into his neck. He flinched and pulled away from her.

"Fuck off, Will! Racine can kiss my ass. I'm not doping some guy because she's got her panties in a wad," Gage growled. He liked Quinn. Quinn never treated Gage like he didn't matter. Everyone else did, forgetting Gage existed half the time. Normally, the youngest was the one coddled, the one that got every ounce of attention. That was entirely the opposite of what happened, though. Bella had all the attention because of who she married. Willow was next because of 'all her health problems'. The only health problem Willow had was being made of plastic.

"You're going to do what I tell you or I'm telling mom and dad what you do in your room at night," Willow hissed, coming close enough for him to smell the liquor on her breath. She was drunk and probably high, knowing Willow. Everyone had their vices. Maybe not Quinn, but he was gay, so he supposed that counted.

Gage merely sighed, refusing to rise to his sister's baiting anymore. He didn't *want* to hurt anyone. However, he also didn't want his parents learning about his habit either. He was working on it. Mostly.

"Good boy," Willow said, caressing his face in that creepy way that made Gage's skin crawl. She left him alone after that, sashaying back to the festivities. Gage watched her go, his eyes landing on Mackenzie loitering just out of sight, ducking back inside when he saw her.

"Fuck me..." Gage sighed, grinding out his cigarette as if it were Willow's cursed head.

#

"Seriously, Angel, how much more of this do we have to do? My face hurts," Quinn grumbled. Angel merely shook his head, throwing a look at Leti and Rachel. The two women offered looks of sympathy in return.

"I'd say until you get it right, *papi*," Leti said. "You kiss like my Tio Niko."

Angel snorted a laugh. Their Tio Niko had very thin lips and always puckered them like he was trying to kiss a fish. The girls sat on the sofa in the bridal suite, offering pointers on Level 3 so that the kisses wouldn't *only* be chaste or look like it was the first time Angel and Quinn were doing so. In theory, they'd been happily ensorcelled with each other for six blissful years. And, while Angel had been happy living with Quinn, what the Langs and their guests were expecting was entirely different from reality.

"You kiss him then," Quinn said, throwing himself on the bed.

"Gross. He's my brother. I don't wanna kiss my brother like that, Quinn. *You* do," Leti threw back.

A soft knock at the door had all of them whipping their heads around in panic. They looked at each other, mouthing questions at each other or trying to decide where people should place themselves.

"Uncle Quinn?"

Quinn visibly sagged when he heard the voice. He got up off the bed and walked to the door.

"It's just my niece," he told everyone as he let the little girl in. She slipped just inside the door with her Switch in hand. When she saw everyone in the room, she offered a little wave.

"Hi," she said. Angel waved back at her.

"Uhm... this is Mackenzie. Elliott's kid. Mackie, that is Rachel, Leti, and this is Angel, my fiancé," Quinn said, looking at Angel as if asking if that was ok. Angel gave him a wink in response. It was progress in the right direction.

"Dad says you make video games," Mackenzie said to Quinn, turning to face him. He smiled at her, bending to be at her level.

"I do," he said.

"Do you wanna play?" she asked. Angel watched Rachel and Leti gush in that silent way that only women could pull off.

"I didn't bring my Switch, Mackie," Quinn said, offering a look that suggested he was genuinely disappointed.

"I brought mine," Angel said, moving to fish it out of his duffel bag. Mackenzie's smile split her face in half.

Rachel and Leti watched while Angel and Quinn took turns trying to beat this little girl at Mario Kart. She was better than Angel, but Quinn gave her a good run for her video game money. The girl played with them until her mother came looking for her at an hour that was unacceptable for a child to be awake. No one in the room had noticed.

"Sorry, Paige," Quinn managed as the woman took her daughter away. Mackenzie seemed to look at them with sad, pleading eyes.

"Get a little more responsibility, Quinn. She's not a video game that runs all night," Paige clipped in return, letting the door slam in her wake. Quinn flinched.

"Then why she didn't come up and say something sooner?" Leti said with full Mexican sass in her words.

"It is late though, we should let the guys get some sleep," Rachel said. Everyone agreed, also agreeing that more practice on Level 3 was needed to make it believable. Quinn sagged, something Angel caught on to, but did not comment on until after the girls had gone.

"Hey–" Angel started but Quinn cut him off.

"We should keep practicing unless you're tired," Quinn sighed. Angel *was* tired, but he also knew they needed to make this look good or all of them were going to be royally fucked.

09

Quinn looked at himself in the mirror, sucked in his gut, and held it.

"What are you doing?" Angel asked as he walked by, fiddling with his bow tie. Quinn let his breath go and sagged, turning to Angel with a pout.

"Do I have a beer belly?"

"What?" Angel laughed. Quinn waited. "What? No, Q, you do not have a beer belly. You'd have to drink more beer for that to happen. Don't let them get to you so much. Argh! *Why does this piece of shit need to have a bow-tie!*"

The last part of Angel's statement was growled in Spanish. Quinn huffed and grabbed the silk cloth his so-called fiancé was fighting with. It came as second nature to tie the beastly things, even if it had been fifteen years since he wore one himself. It was like riding a bike – Quinn's hands just knew how to make the stupid thing work. He kept his focus on the tie until it was done, smoothing it against Angel's collarbones before realizing what he was doing.

"Sorry," he said, quickly turning away.

"For what? You're supposed to be doing things like that, remember? Level 2. I thought we got past that part?" Angel said, looking over Quinn's head at the bowtie. "How'd you do that?"

"Practice. A lot of it," Quinn shrugged. He still wouldn't look at Angel. Their outfits matched in complimenting colors that had subtle rainbows in it. Angel's had it on the bowtie, Quinn's on the lapel. Both wore rainbow-colored cufflinks and socks. It was so over the top Quinn wanted to vomit. "So, no talking about your job. Your parents don't like white people – thank Leti for that one. You work for a small law-firm in DC."

"Why do we have to lie about our relationship *and* my job?" Angel pouted. Quinn wanted to kiss him and hold him forever. "I like my job."

"I know, I know, but my dad won't," Quinn pleaded. "Please. Angel, please."

"Fine," Angel sighed, then glowered. "But only because it's fifty million and I'm in Italy with all the booze I want."

Quinn nodded, then went back to the mirror. He recited his anxiety mantras *eight times* before Angel finally came up behind him, hands on shoulders.

"Level 3, Quinn. It's just a game," Angel encouraged. "Breathe. You slay monsters for a living. Slay them. You got this."

Quinn nodded, reaching up to put a hand on Angel's without thinking. Angel didn't pull away, offering an encouraging grin instead.

Out in the vineyard, several long tables were set out with crisp white linens and pale pastel bows in rainbow colors on the chairs. A spray of wildflowers sat in small bowls at even intervals across the long tables with tall candles in the same pale rainbows as the bows to either side of the wildflowers.

"Oh, yay! Ok, ok, come here, both of you," Bella said. She grabbed both Quinn and Angel like they were her children, dragging them to a small fountain not far from where the long tables were set up. "Stand there. Just like yesterday. Oh, here."

Bella shoved a soft velvet box at Quinn. Quinn looked at it, opened it, then frowned. "Bells, I have a ring."

"Oh, right, Angel proposed," Bella corrected, snatching the box from Quinn to shove it at Angel. "We're doing actual engagement photos. Like, the proposing ones."

Both men stared at Bella like she'd gone mad.

"I already proposed," Angel hazarded.

Quinn nodded, pointing at Angel. "What he said."

"Yeah, but no one saw it. So you need to do it again," Bella explained. Quinn merely sighed, hearing Angel do the same.

The Langs made dinner an affair to remember; again. Quinn started seeing spots from all the photos taken. He worried about Angel, worried about how the flash bulbs might affect him, but he handled it well. By the time it was all over, Quinn wanted to launch himself into the Mediterranean.

Sadly, such things were not allowed. His mother cornered him to complain about Angel's missing family and how that made *her* look followed by another 'discussion' with his father. Quinn watched everyone else slip away while he got earful after earful, shuffling back up the stairs over an hour after dinner concluded. Angel was sitting on the couch in their suite, talking to Mackenzie.

"Hi, uncle Quinn."

"Oh, hey, Mackenzie. What's up?"

"This room is the quietest. I asked Angel if I

could sit in here for a while. I'll leave you guys alone though so mom doesn't yell at me again," she said, standing up with her phone and Switch in hand. "Night."

"Night," Quinn said with Angel echoing him. Angel smiled, looking at Quinn, new adoration in his brown eyes. Angel loved kids.

"She's cute. Ten?"

"Yeah, I think so."

"She's going to give you a run for your money on those games," Angel said, standing so he could stretch, shirt rucking up just enough to show off that amazing V dipping into his sweats. "She said she wants to be a zookeeper though so we'll see maybe–"

Quinn swallowed Angel's words with an open-mouth kiss Angel was *not* expecting. Quinn's hands came up to hold Angel's face, making sure he would not move or pull away. Angel didn't even know how to react to it. He'd never kissed a guy like that before. In fact, the only guy he'd kissed before Quinn was one of their mutual friends on a dare that got him a hundred dollars and a free bed. This was not anything like that, nor like anything they'd been practicing. His stomach tightened painfully, and all of his muscles seized all at once. Quinn deepened the kiss, tongue seeking

Angel's while Angel's muscles continued to spasm.

Then, Angel melted.

He couldn't even explain it. Feeling Quinn's tongue against his own, the way Quinn held his face, it made something inside him snap and every muscle liquefy. He even held on to Quinn's shoulders so he wouldn't fall to the floor from becoming so insanely weak-kneed. It was the exact opposite of the seizure he was expecting. In fact, it was like a scene right out of a romance movie. He was turning into a dammed romance movie!

They kissed like that until Angel literally could not breathe anymore and pushed Quinn back enough to gasp. "Ok, slow down a minute..."

"Sorry. Honestly, I don't know why I did that. I just... acted. It's been such a shitty night and it's only day two and I want to die, I needed something *good*. I'm...I'm sorry."

"It's ok. I'm..." Angel said, still holding tight to Quinn's arms so he wouldn't fall over. Quinn guided him back down to the couch, sitting beside him. "Uhm... wow."

Quinn laughed, raking a hand through his hair. Angel felt like he'd just been hit with a two by four. Level 3 *definitely* achieved.

Angel took a minute to calm himself, to steady his breathing, and study Quinn's face. It was flushed from the kiss and the emotions he was positive they were *both* feeling. Things got so weird after Quinn's parents made their visit, weirder still after Quinn's confession, and they'd only been in Italy for three whirlwind days. It could just be the rush of living a lie, or something more. It was hard for Angel to tell. He knew for certain that he did not like the uncomfortable silence between them. So, he leaned forward and captured Quinn in another kiss that made Quinn moan a little in the back of his throat.

That was all they did for the longest time. They made out, exploring everything above the waist with experimental gropes done over their pants. Angel had never been with a man either. By the way Quinn was fumbling around, he imagined what the Asian man said was true and not just some awkward ploy. It was ... odd. Almost like they were teenagers experimenting for the first time, minus the hesitation. Because Angel had no hesitation. That was probably the most surprising thing of all.

Angel didn't really have a preference for one gender over another. He enjoyed sex *with Rachel,* but never actively sought it out. Rachel was the one that invited him over and he genuinely enjoyed her company because of her *heart.* It was *Quinn* that now seemed to complicate things,

Quinn that had Angel hard in his sweats and so desperate for the other man's touch it hurt. *Quinn* made his heart beat so fast in his rib-cage he had to force himself to calm down or induce a seizure – just like Rachel had when they first got together. Just like Rachel *still* did, he realized.

"Are you ok?" Quinn breathed, kissing down Angel's neck. Angel nodded. "If you want me to stop…"

"No," Angel assured him. "No, keep going."

If they weren't so caught up in the moment, their actions might be comical. Quinn kissed his way down Angel's chest to the V that dipped into his sweatpants before tugging them off, boxers and all. He kissed the inside of Angel's thigh, then took Angel into his mouth.

"Oh, shit!" Angel gasped, hands immediately flying to Quinn's head. He watched Quinn bob up and down his length, swirling his tongue or giving loud sucks. It was, by and large, the absolute worst blowjob he'd ever had, but it was *Quinn* doing it. It didn't matter how awful it was. Angel was so hot he was cumming down Quinn's throat in just a few short sucks.

"Ok, you're either really horny or I did a really good job," Quinn laughed, wiping his mouth with the back of his hand.

"Shut up, Quinn," Angel said, tugging

the other man back up to a smoldering kiss. He fumbled blindly for Quinn's pants, kicking those down with his feet until they were both naked, making out like horny college kids.

Angel took Quinn in hand, stroking gently to illicit that glorious whimper he'd heard when they first kissed. It worked.

That was how the night passed: touching and kissing, caressing or giving terrible blowjobs that got better as the night progressed. By the time morning rolled around, they were both nestled beneath the downy soft blankets, with Quinn tucked into Angel's chest, both so exhausted they slept clear through breakfast.

No one noticed.

Levels 4 and 5 achieved.

#

Rachel walked through the castle alone, dodging guests left and right. A light breeze blew through the entirety of the large limestone edifice, swirling the linen dress she wore around her ankles. She and Leti had shopped with the boys – a gift from Quinn so they would all look good in front of his parents. The dress she wore cost two hundred dollars. Despite the sticker shock, it was one of the most comfortable things she'd ever worn. Not that the price tag had prevented the other guests from whispering about how cheap it was – or her weight.

Clothing aside, the entire thing was starting to feel grossly overwhelming. She could only imagine what Angel and Quinn were going through. Everywhere she went, Rachel felt like she was being watched, or peered at by the others at the 'party'. Even that seemed over the top. It wasn't just *one* party, but many rolled into one long, Italian getaway. The glitz and glamor of it all was breathtaking. Yet, despite all the 'fun', Rachel very desperately wanted to go home.

Instead, Rachel threw herself down on the bed in her room. Hers did not have a balcony like Angel and Quinn's did, but it was still twice the size of her normal bedroom and connected to Leti's by a shared Jack-and-Jill bathroom that was also twice the size of anything normal. A gentle knock on her door lifted her head up with curiosity.

"Rae? You in here?" Angel asked from the other side. She'd know his voice anywhere. She felt a grin spread across her lips as she got up to open the door. Angel looked back at her with exhaustion painting his handsome face. "Mind if I hide for a little bit?"

"Come on in," she said, opening the door enough to allow him entry. She glanced around to make sure no one saw, almost as an afterthought, then decided she didn't care anymore and shut the door. "You ok?"

Angel nodded, but then huffed and shrugged, falling face first onto her bed. He groaned, making her smirk. "Where's Q?"

"Getting an earful from his parents about us missing breakfast yesterday. The guests are 'talking'," Angel said, face still in the soft comforter while raising his arms high enough to make air quotes. Rachel's smirk spread into a smile. She went to him, crawling onto the bed first, then straddling his bottom so she could rub his shoulders. It made him groan.

"You're stressed. I feel it in your shoulders," Rachel said to him. He snorted into the comforter.

"You'd be stressed, too," he replied in muffled tones. "God, that feels good."

Rachel continued rubbing Angel's shoulders. One tense spot at a time, she got the muscles to loosen up, got the man lying beneath her to relax and just breathe in silence for a few blessed minutes.

"What did I do to deserve you?" Angel asked as he finally rolled over. She rolled with him, swinging off his bottom to stretch out beside him instead.

"Beat up a handsy asshole on the Metro for me," she grinned, tucking a lock of hair behind his ear. He smiled back, making her heart swell while her stomach knotted. None of this was as fake as the boys claimed it was. They were both as smitten by each other as Rachel was by Angel. Everyone saw it – *especially* Rachel.

"What?" Angel asked when Rachel stared too long. She looked away from his face, steeling herself against what was to come. "Rae?"

"Kiss me?" she said instead of speaking her mind. She regretted it as soon as the request left her lips, feeling like she was betraying Quinn or being selfish in asking Angel to shower *her* with attention, too. What hurt more was the fact that he didn't deny her. He did exactly as she asked, pulling her close to kiss her tenderly. It took her breath away. She shivered when he ran fingers through her hair, then shivered again when Angel adjusted their positions so he half hovered above her, half laid beside her.

"God, Angel…" she breathed against his lips. Angel swallowed her words with another kiss that carried far more passion in it than it should have. They were in Italy, for *his* wedding to someone *else*! Somewhere in Rachel's mind, her coherent, logical self screamed at the part that reveled in Angel's touch and coveted everything he gave her.

His hand slid beneath the linen dress she wore, drawing it up to her thighs. She wore nothing beneath it, testing the feel of something so expensive against her bare skin. She was glad of it now, easily relieving Angel of any fabric burdens he had, crying out into his open mouth when he slid inside of her.

They moved together on the bed, moaning softly into each other's mouths. Rachel's hands made their way beneath Angel's shirt, loosening some of the buttons so she could touch every sculpted muscle, tracing the tattoos she'd had memorized mere months after meeting him. What they did seemed wrong, and yet entirely what they *should* be doing in a lavish resort in *Italy*. God knew everyone else in this horrid family had their secrets and vices. What was one more?

Even thinking that put a seed of self-loathing in Rachel's stomach. She did not want to think ill of Quinn. He was the one being tormented by the hideous people that called him family. She didn't have to be told why he and Angel were not at breakfast. It wasn't that hard to figure out. She knew how much Angel loved Quinn even if Angel didn't – yet. So Rachel took what she could, while she could, and prayed she never needed to be far from Angel Rivera for any reason.

#

Angel looked down at himself, then looked over at Quinn later that evening. He felt his face flush some, then looked away. They decided that Level 4 was their new comfort zone, now sharing the bed rather than sleeping separately, but nothing further happened between them beyond Level 4 after that single night. Their kisses were now one hundred percent believable, but everything else felt a little awkward all of a sudden. The outfits for the evening involved elaborate costumes that Angel *knew* cost more than his salary.

Jewels and rhinestones decorated the lapel of a velvet coat with tails for himself. There was a half mask to go with it made to look like a sugar skull. Quinn had one in blues and purples to match the peacock feathers on his coat. It was absurd, but cool at the same time.

"She really put all of this together to show off?" Angel asked while still adjusting the *cravat* around his neck. He didn't even know what the stupid thing was called until Quinn told him. It made him feel like he was choking.

"Not sure how you've missed that so far," Quinn replied as he fiddled with his cufflinks. "Everything she does is to show off."

Angel merely nodded and then sighed. "Things got weird again, Q." Quinn stopped what he was doing as if being struck with an ice ray. "Quinn?"

"I'm not trying to make it weird," he sighed. "I just... I dunno. I... I don't even know how to process any of this Angel. I'm marrying you, but not marrying you, and we're totally sharing a bed and stuff but..."

"But?" Angel prompted, moving to stand next to Quinn.

"But what happens when we go home?" he finished. Quinn didn't worry about things like that. The man thought in the immediate twenty-four hours and very little beyond that. It was the reason Angel made sure bills got paid and things on their calendar got updated regularly.

"I don't know, Q. I didn't think we *had* to know. This is literally crazy new to both of us."

"For you," Quinn whined. "I've been pining for you since college! And what about Rachel!"

"What about me?" she asked. Angel and Quinn both jumped. "Sorry. Leti sent me to make sure you weren't tied up in your ties. Everything ok?"

"Yeah, fine," Angel said. He found himself dumbstruck by Rachel's costume. The gown was low cut, with a corset that enhanced every part of her. Her fair skin was covered in a fine dusting of glitter and hair done up in an intricate up-do. She held a mask in her gloved hands that looked crocheted from lace.

"You look amazing," Angel said recalling what they'd done that afternoon. She smiled and blushed making her even more beautiful.

"So do you," she replied, then added. "You do too, Q. Love the feathers."

"Thanks," Quinn said, sounding defeated.

"Give us a minute?" Angel whispered to Rachel. She nodded and left them alone to talk. "Quinn?"

The man looked at Angel with sad resignation in his dark brown eyes. "I'm fine."

"But you're not. I've known you long enough to know when you're pouting; when you're *not* fine. What's wrong?"

"Nothing," Quinn insisted. "I'm ok. We should go before mom comes in to shove me into that torture device again."

Quinn moved around Angel. Angel sighed and let it go. It wasn't worth the headache he was getting to press Quinn further. He followed, going down to the opulence of the masquerade ball already in session.

Bulbs flashed in their faces as they smiled, posed, kissed, and played this sick game everyone wanted to see.

*Fifty **million** dollars,* Angel thought, repeating it over and over as he swam through the throngs of masked guests with a knot building up in his stomach the rest of the night.

10

The castle boasted acreage that had everything: from vineyards, to horse paddocks, to little creeks that went to hidden springs. It was the most magical place Angel had ever been. He and Rachel agreed to meet at the stables for a break from the insanity following the masquerade. Every night, the Langs planned some sort of dinner, or ball, or event to 'celebrate' the coming nuptials. Guests were encouraged to enjoy the grounds but expected to attend dinner in a new outfit like models on a runway – hence the twenty-two matching outfits Quinn and Angel had. So, to just breathe, they came out to pet the horses. Angel fed one of them carrots and apples while Rachel brushed it out. It was soothing.

"Where did you learn to do that?" Angel asked. Rachel shrugged. She still wore the fake lashes that made her eyes look stunning the night before.

"Summer camp. Ever been on a horse?" Angel shook his head. She smiled. "Have you talked to Quinn?"

Angel paused, patting the horse's nose gently, and looked at his friend and lover. Thinking about her like that made his stomach whirl, but not as much as thinking about Quinn did. That was a new sensation that complicated matters. "I talk to him every day."

"No, I mean about what's going on," Rachel clarified. Angel felt heat rush to his face and that giddy whirl turn into a knot. Rachel noticed.

"Good," she smiled. "I was hoping I wasn't going to have to be the one to tell you."

"Tell me what?"

"What you just realized," Rachel smiled. "Try to let him know I'm not a threat, either, ok? He seemed upset last night when I went to check on you."

"Rae," Angel started, but didn't know how to continue. When the words finally formed in his mind, he tried again. "I'm not sure what's happening with Quinn. It's really weird, but that doesn't change how I feel about you, you know?"

"I know," she nodded. Her voice sounded sad and resigned. It broke Angel's heart. He wanted to say more, mouth opening to do so, but he stopped when Leti joined them. Guilt hit him so hard he felt dizzy.

"These guys are so beautiful, aren't you?" Leti cooed at the horse. Angel smirked and shook his head – and kept shaking it.

"Angel!" Leti said, getting his attention. He felt light-headed suddenly and had his hand fisted in the horse's mane. The horse did not seem bothered by it.

"Yeah..?" He muttered. He was aware of Leti massaging his hand and Rachel massaging his back when he heard the cackling snicker of another woman.

"Cheating already? Usually they wait until after the honeymoon, gardener trash."

"Excuse me?" Leti said. Angel wanted to stop her, but couldn't think straight. "Who the fuck are you?"

"Leti, don't," Rachel warned, now holding Angel's hand so he could lean into her. He felt tired suddenly and disoriented. He was having a seizure. "Look, whatever your problem is, it can wait. We just want to get Angel back to the castle," Rachel said. The woman snorted.

"Private three-way with the help?"

"Listen, *puta*," Leti started. Angel absently reached for her, then felt himself fall forward into spasms. When he woke, he was back in the castle with Quinn sitting at his side. He could hear Rachel and Leti too, both complaining about the woman at the stables.

"You ok?" Quinn whispered, taking Angel's hand in his. Angel nodded. "I'll let them know."

Quinn left his side for a moment before returning.

"Elliott came by to look at you," Quinn explained. "He said it was just minor. Probably from all the stuff going on. He told mom to back off for a couple days."

Angel snorted, grinning a little. He slept until the next morning, waking with Quinn curled up beside him. Angel did not immediately get up, just watching his 'fiancé' sleep. He would watch Rachel sleep in the same way sometimes. Thinking about her reminded him of the conversation they'd been having before his seizure. He didn't want to hurt her *or* Quinn.

It was a problem for another time. Angel slipped out of bed, standing beneath scalding hot water to clear his mind, relax his muscles, and recenter his soul. He reminded himself why he was putting up with Quinn's stupid family, then remembered that he also *enjoyed* the night of awkward exploration with Quinn. Maybe being married to him wouldn't be so bad. He could certainly do worse than a person he had absolute trust in.

"Angel?"

Angel turned toward the sound of Quinn's voice. The other man hovered in the doorway to the bathroom, letting some of the steam out.

"How are you feeling?"

"Better. Needed a shower," Angel answered, turning the water off. He stepped out with no towel, smirking when Quinn looked down at the floor and flushed. "Quinn, you've had my dick in your mouth. You can look."

"Do you really have to say it like that?" Quinn sighed. "Ass. Look, uhm... Elliott made everyone go out on the yacht today so we could have the castle mostly to ourselves. There's a few people still around but, it'll be quiet if you want to go back out to the stables or the springs. I think Leti and Rachel stayed behind. Or if you want to go with Ra–"

Angel cut Quinn off with a gentle kiss, holding his chin between his thumb and pointer finger. Quinn responded by wrapping his arms around Angel's damp back, fingers pressing into the muscle.

"I don't need to go with Rachel," Angel rumbled. "She knows. And I can't ride horses so... maybe the springs, instead. Or we can just stay here and get room service like a normal vacation."

"Angel, we're in Italy. We can get room service in DC," Quinn countered without letting go. Angel sighed, backing up a step. Quinn finally let go, looking to the side so he wouldn't be looking at Angel's crotch.

"Fine, the springs then," Angel chortled, grabbing a towel so Quinn would stop averting his eyes.

They *did* order room service first though, enjoying a nice breakfast on their balcony before taking a hike to the hidden springs. A brief inquiry told them the girls had gone on a tour of the local town, which left Angel and Quinn alone for the day. It was probably better that way. They needed to talk.

"You're having second thoughts, aren't you?" Quinn said once they were both nestled in the warm, bubbling springs. Angel relaxed against a stone, eyes closed.

"No," he answered without moving. "Who is that banshee that was coming for me like I killed her kitten? She was bitching the other night, too. I remembered her voice."

"Racine Fier," Quinn replied. "She's the one I'm *supposed* to be marrying. She'll come at you until you give up or die."

"Good to know," Angel snickered. "She's a

bitch. You would really marry that if your dad told you to?"

Silence.

Angel lifted his head up so he could look at Quinn. The other man had his eyes focused on the clear water.

"Q, have you talked to anyone about this? You have some serious issues with your dad. You're an adult. He *can't* actually make you do anything you don't want."

"Yes, he can," Quinn replied in a near rasp. "He can take everything I love to force me to comply."

"Really? He'd take everything just to make you marry some crazy ass bitch in stilettos? For what? What does *he* get out of it?"

"Stature," Quinn answered without a moment's thought. "Every move is to gain respect, wealth, status, rich people clout. Why do you think I was praying he'd just disown me when he found out I was gay?"

Angel sighed, leaning back again. The silence intensified to uncomfortable, nearly rage–inducing levels. Angel hated it, hated the feel of that tension between them. The poor man looked miserable and beyond defeated; like a beat puppy. Angel moved to Quinn's side and bumped his shoulder.

"Talk to me," Angel encouraged.

Silence.

"Q."

"I don't want to lose you, Angel," Quinn finally said. "You're my best friend. You're more than that. We share a *bathroom* for fuck's sake."

Angel let out a laugh through his nose, but did not stop Quinn's train of thought otherwise.

"I just feel like all of this is going to mess us up. That we'll do this and go home and be different people and... I don't want that. It sounds so lame, but you mean everything to me and I'm watching my stupid family find a new way to tear that apart. Fuck, I'm surprised you've only had *one* seizure. The pictures alone would give *me* one."

Angel snorted. The pictures *were* a bit over the top. But so was everything else.

"And what about Rachel? And don't you dare tell me there's nothing between you two because there is, Angel, *everyone* sees it. Christ, my *mom* asked what was with you two. I just, I dunno... maybe it would be better if I do what my dad says."

Now Angel frowned. He moved so he could be directly in front of Quinn and made sure the Asian idiot could not look away.

"*That*," Angel said firmly. "Is not an option. *We* are getting married. I may not even know what that means right now, but we're doing it. *We are going to have a lovely honeymoon in a castle all to ourselves, and we will figure the rest out later. I told you Rachel knows that I have feelings for you. You know I'm feeling something for you.* I wouldn't have let you do what we did if I didn't have feelings for you. Maybe we'll invite Rachel to be our third. But *right now*, she's here to support *us*. So is my sister, and that's all we need. You with me?"

Quinn listened, jaw a little slack, then finally nodded with a sheen of tears in his eyes that broke Angel's heart. How far down had he been beaten to be willing to give up so easily?

"Don't cry," Angel sighed. Quinn scrubbed his face with his arm.

"M'not," he muttered. Angel pulled him into a hug, letting Quinn fall apart.

#

"Mmmmm I definitely liked that wine better than the first one we tried," Rachel said as she relaxed in a wrought-iron chair that overlooked cobblestone streets and little cafes.

She and Leti let the boys have some much-needed 'alone time' while they extracted themselves from Lang insanity by taking a trip around the beautiful city they were in. None of the other guests seemed to care that they were in *Italy*, or that the immaculate art and history of the world was literally at their fingertips.

"I do too. This place is so beautiful. I really wish my parents could've come. They would love to see Angel get married like this," Leti said, then paused and looked at Rachel. "You know, everyone was rooting for you, right?"

"Rooting for me?" Rachel asked, dropping her sunglasses to the tip of her nose. She wore a wide-brimmed hat, allowing herself to pretend to be one of the catty rich bitches present for the wedding without the bitchiness. Leti did the same, sticking her nose in the air like Julia Roberts in *Pretty Woman*.

"For Angel to marry you," Leti explained. "My *abuelita* is always asking about the nice plump girl."

"Plump!" Rachel barked through a stifled laugh. Leti giggled in return. Rachel was not a rail. She had curves that others found off-putting. Angel didn't. He loved her curves, loved her from her head to her painted little toes. She knew it as surely as she knew he loved Quinn the same way.

"My *abuelita* loves you. She's always asking about you, saying what a good match you are for her *'Angelito'* and what beautiful babies you'd make. She's so weird sometimes, and old."

Rachel smiled kindly but didn't comment further, taking another sip of her delicious wine instead. She wasn't a good match for Angel. Asking him to marry her was selfish, done out of pure loneliness. She couldn't give him what he wanted most, but she wanted to pretend for a little while. Not that Quinn could give Angel what he wanted either. At least, on that, they were even. What Angel was doing with Quinn changed things. It broke her heart a little, but she tried her best not to let it show.

"She'll just have to be happy with whoever Quinn and Angel adopt, I guess," Rachel deflected after a moment of self-pity.

"It really doesn't bother you? What they're doing?" Leti asked. Rachel looked at her, studied how much this woman looked like Angel, spoke like him, moved like him. They were definitely related. Rachel didn't have siblings. Her parents decided one was enough and filled the rest of their lives with animals in need. It was why Rachel worked where she did, felt so passionately about what they fought for.

"No," Rachel finally answered. "Seems sudden, and weird, kinda, but it doesn't bother me. I've known Quinn was Angel's house husband from the first day I met him. That's how he introduced me to Quinn – 'this is my house husband, Quinn'. But... I know it may have *started* as sort of a money grab, but that's not what it is anymore.

Angel really cares about Quinn, worries how his family treats him. I'm pretty sure he loves the big oaf but hasn't admitted it to himself yet."

"He loves you too," Leti pointed out. Rachel smiled, blessed to have this woman on her side.

"I know."

11

Water lapped over Angel's body as he glided through the warmth of the heated pool. The temperature relaxed his muscles while the activity kept him focused. It had been three more trying days of posing, measurements for the next outfit, more fake and forced dinners. Fake wedding or not, it should be something fun, not all the work they were having to put in. Things got *worse* between Angel and Quinn in the privacy of their own room, despite their talk in the springs. They'd fooled around a little more, with Angel actually doing most of the work while Quinn tried not to pout or freak out anytime he heard someone near their door. Part of Angel just wanted to fuck and be done with it, although the other part was afraid it would make things weirder still. Quinn had so much repressed anxiety with his parents that needed to be worked out, something that would not happen while the 'rents were present.

When he came up for air, the sight of feet at the edge of the pool made him stop and wipe his face of the chlorinated water to look up. Quinn stood there, looking down at him.

"Hey," Quinn said.

"Hey," Angel blew out, scrubbing the water from his face. "Did I miss another social event?"

"After dinner brandy, yeah," Quinn said. "Don't worry about it. I didn't go either. I snuck out with Mackenzie. We got ice cream."

"Oh, good. Someone needs to pay attention to that poor kid," Angel said, then bit his tongue. "Sorry..."

Mackenzie broke Angel's heart as much as Quinn did. No one seemed to notice how lonely she was. Quinn only shrugged, gliding down to a squat, so he was closer to Angel. "Can we talk? Just... no stress, no weirdness, just... talk?"

Angel nodded, climbing out of the pool so he could dry off. Quinn followed, hands stuffed into his pockets and eyes fastened to his feet. "Q, what's wrong?"

Quinn shrugged. "Nothing, I just... I dunno."

Angel moved closer, towel hanging over his shoulder. Water dripped down his legs to his feet, making little splashing noises as he padded over to Quinn. "I thought we were going to talk? Hell, I thought we *did* talk. What happened?"

"We were," Quinn muttered. "Are. We are. And, we did, but... I talked to my dad earlier and..."

"Quinn?" Angel persisted. Quinn looked up, looking decidedly miserable. "Strip."

"What?" Quinn intoned.

"You heard me. Strip," Angel said, snatching another towel from the bin to toss at Quinn. It hit Quinn in the face, making Angel roll his eyes as he stepped out of his saturated swim trunks and wrapped his towel around his waist. He waited for Quinn to do the same, then dragged the man into the sauna. Sweat immediately made them both slick and plastered hair to their heads.

The warmth inside the spacious cedar room was a drastic difference from the pool, making the pool seem like ice. Angel sat first, doffing the towel to the side, then pulled Quinn into his lap in such a manner that Quinn's towel fell to the floor. Quinn froze.

"Angel..."

"Relax, Q. Just sit and relax," Angel whispered. "I'm just here to hold you and listen. Do what you feel you need to. Let the sauna relax your shoulders a little. You're too tense."

Quinn remained a stiff board for a few more

moments, then finally leaned his head against Angel's shoulder, hands holding on to Angel's tattooed arms.

"I hate this," Quinn whispered. "Dad was talking about Racine again and asking if I was *really* gay or just pretending so I didn't have to marry her and... I just wanna go home."

Angel rubbed Quinn's back, kissing Quinn's neck. "Then we'll go home. Blame me. Say I'm not feeling well. You don't need to stay here and put up with this shit, Q."

"I do. So you can buy your mom a house."

"Quinn, it's money. And it isn't worth your misery. Ok? We'll leave."

Skin to skin, in such a vulnerable position, Angel merely continued to lavish Quinn with kisses and encouragements until the man finally, blessedly *relaxed*. When Quinn looked up, there was a different look on his face that had Angel's stomach knotting again. Quinn leaned in to kiss him, something gentle and probing, then more insistent. Angel returned it in kind, holding Quinn closer, tighter. He let Quinn know how excited he was, his dick hard and slick with pre-cum beneath Quinn's slightly spread ass. Angel could feel Quinn's too, trapped between them and pulsing. He let his hands wander, let them squeeze Quinn's ass cheeks and then tease his hole with a single finger, grinning when Quinn shuddered.

"Oh... fuck, Angel..."

"If you'll let me," Angel purred, looking Quinn in the eye while teasing, circling until he could slip that finger inside Quinn. The look of surprise and joy was worth every ounce of hell his family was giving them. "Please let me, Quinn."

Quinn nodded so hard and so fast Angel thought his head might pop off. The kiss that followed was rough and desperate, pleading in its own way. He knew they couldn't stay in the sauna. Someone might see and supplies were needed, or their first time was going to cause more irreparable damage to Quinn's well-being.

"Come back upstairs with me," Angel said in a husky voice against Quinn's neck. Quinn nodded again, leading the way with Angel's hand in his. They hit their room faster than expected, dropping them back into that horrible awkward silence from before.

Angel resumed their original positions, sitting on the bed instead of a sauna bench, pulling Quinn into his lap to just hold his friend, to touch him, and make him feel *loved* for what was probably the first time in his life. He felt the tension in Quinn's arms and shoulders, his back, all of it so tightly wound he was sure Quinn would snap at any second. So, Angel didn't press. Whatever lust that built up between them in the sauna dissipated between there and the bridal suite.

"I love you," Angel said, knowing Quinn wouldn't believe him. "No matter what happens or how crazy your family gets, I love you. Understand?"

Quinn remained silent for a long time, then finally lifted his head off Angel's shoulder and looked him in the eye. Angel met the look, *showing* Quinn he wasn't playing any game. He knew there were several meanings behind that single word, love, and perhaps he was still figuring them all out with Quinn, but he loved his friend, from top to bottom and every quirky thing in between. He didn't expect a response back. That wasn't the kind of person Quinn was.

"Please, just kiss me," Quinn finally said. Angel watched him swallow that fear, his Adam's apple bobbing up and down. Angel gave Quinn what he needed. He pulled Quinn close, kissing him gently, with love and compassion. His fingers explored Quinn's body like they'd been doing in the sauna, but without the lust-filled urgency. Angel let Quinn set the pace, responding as the lust between them grew again until he was slowly spreading Quinn's cheeks open to tease again. Quinn groaned into the kiss, all the muscles unwinding with that one touch.

Much like everything else, they took their time, exploring and playing with each other, laughing when the lube got a little too slippery between them. Angel got three fingers inside Quinn before the other man finally gave in.

"God, Angel, I need you so much! Please! Fuck!" Quinn squeaked, his voice pitched so high it cracked. Angel smiled, trying not to laugh, even if he felt the same.

"Trust me," Angel reminded Quinn, "and relax."

Angel kissed Quinn, helping the man shift on his lap so he was lined up to accept Angel's overly lubed-up cock. Angel moved painfully slow, not wanting to hurt his friend or ruin the moment. He let Quinn guide him, massaging Quinn's ass as the other man settled over the tip of Angel's cock, then pressed down until the head popped inside.

The tightness was mind-blowing. Angel nearly orgasmed from that alone, groaning deep against Quinn's neck. Quinn had stopped breathing, fingers pressing painfully into Angel's shoulders.

"Breathe, Quinn," Angel reminded, "Please breathe, relax. I won't hurt you, I promise. Not ever."

"Oh, fuck..." Quinn finally breathed as he slid down, inch by inch until he was sitting all the way in

Angel's lap again. "Jesus, Angel!"

"Shhh..." Angel said, kissing Quinn's brow. He smoothed the other man's hair back from his sweaty face, giving him sweet, innocent kisses as he cooed gently. "God, Q, you feel so *good*."

Quinn did not reply with words but with noises of mixed pleasure and pain. He remained quiet and still for a time, leaning against Angel's shoulder, then moved his hips enough to let Angel thrust in and out at a gentle, drawn-out pace.

"Tell me if I hurt you," Angel whispered, reveling in one of the most amazing sexual experiences he'd ever had. He wanted to feel it for himself, tempted to switch just so he *could* feel it.

"Keep going," Quinn whispered, then looked up at Angel. "Please. Keep going."

Angel obliged. They didn't speak, kissing each other, touching each other like they'd been doing all night. Angel did everything he could to make Quinn feel good, rocking gently inside of him, caressing Quinn's cock until it was leaking so heavily Angel was sure Quinn would orgasm with the next stroke. Quinn was so tight it was difficult to keep from exploding with each rock or thrust.

"Angel..." Quinn whined. "Angel I... fuck... thrust harder. Thrust harder!"

"Why? Are–"

"Angel!"

"Ok!" Angel replied, adjusting to thrust a little harder, like Quinn wanted. The muscle retracted and sucked Angel in more with each thrust.

"Fuck! Oh, God! Keep going! I'm almost there! Shit!" Quinn cried, holding Angel's hand to his own cock, both of them stroking him off while Angel thrust harder and harder until Quinn exploded between them. "OH SHIT!"

"God... Quinn..." Angel squeaked out, unable to hold back. The last thrust sent Angel over the edge. Both men simply squeaked or groaned, rubbing and stroking, bouncing until they could not move anymore.

"Oh, fuck... oh, fuck... Jesus Christ..." Quinn breathed heavily.

"Don't take the–" Angel started, but Quinn silenced him with an open-mouthed kiss that took all thought from Angel's mind. Angel did not speak again after that. He let Quinn crawl off his lap, watched in awe at how incredibly *hot* it was to see the mess he'd made slide down Quinn's legs.

Angel dropped to his knees after seeing that, pleasuring Quinn to another orgasm, and another, and another. This was not awkward exploration. This was love-making in its purest, most sincere form. He made love to Quinn again, spooning the other man from behind, holding him tight and close. When Quinn was ready, Angel happily gave himself to his longtime friend, biting down on his hand when Quinn entered him for the first time from how *good* it felt. Even with the pain, he wanted it to last forever.

They shared that union until both were spent and exhausted, Angel heaving heavily against Quinn's chest with Quinn still inside him when they realized the sun was rising.

"Breakfast will be served soon," Quinn muttered without moving, idly stroking Angel's back like Rachel would do. It felt *right* to have Quinn do it.

"I don't need breakfast," Angel said through a heavy breath. "I need you."

He caught the hitch in Quinn's breathing and felt the uptick in his heartbeat beneath where he rested his cheek. Angel still didn't move.

"Angel?" Quinn began, already beginning to stir inside of Angel.

"Yeah?" Angel replied. Quinn remained silent. Angel shifted so he could look up, pushing himself down further on Quinn's semi-flaccid cock. "What?"

"Marry me," Quinn finally said, nearly choking on the words. "For real. Marry me? No bullshit, no money. Just me and you."

Angel grinned, kissing Quinn sweetly,

whispering a very gentle, "Yes," against his lips.

"Really?" Quinn whispered back. Angel nodded, smiling when Quinn tucked a sweaty strand of hair behind Angel's ear.

"Still want to go home?" Angel asked. Quinn shrugged. "Then we'll go home."

"They won't let us. Even if you're 'sick'," Quinn murmured. "If we stay, we get free booze and cake."

"Fine," Angel said, capturing Quinn in another deep kiss. "But we're skipping dinner tonight."

"We can't skip dinner," Quinn smirked. Angel growled.

"I'm going to teach you to be independent if it kills me," Angel finished, kissing Quinn hard while tightening his legs around Quinn's hips until Quinn was a rock inside of him again.

No one saw them until dinner.

12

Sunlight glinted off Willow Lang's sunglasses. She stared out over the surrounding vineyards from *her* private balcony, soaking in the sun in little more than a silk robe loosely tied around her perfectly tanned body. She'd heard her brother's nocturnal activities, reporting it to Racine the following morning when the two failed to show up for Marjorie Lang's commanded breakfast. A bottle of champagne sat in a bucket of ice beside her, with five empty ones lined up along the balcony wall.

"Will!"

The sound of Racine's high-pitched screech made Willow sigh. She refused to move, letting the high-strung woman come out to the balcony on her own.

"What are you doing? You're supposed to

be getting rid of this fucker marrying your stupid fag of a brother," the woman snarled.

"Relax, Racey, I'm taking care of it," Willow slurred. "Sit down. Have some champagne."

"How are you taking care of it?" Racine snapped, snatching Willow's champagne flute from her perfectly lacquered fingers. Willow tilted her sunglasses down to glare at Racine.

"Do not forget who you're talking to, Racine Fier – or who *else* has secrets in their closet," Willow threatened as she got up off the lounger to snatch her drink back, squaring off with the other woman.

"The point is the money, Willow, not that he's a fag," Racine hissed between clenched teeth. "We'd literally have to have sex *once* just to get me pregnant and never touch each other again!"

"I know how the inheritance works, Racey," Willow sighed heavily, looking the other woman up and down with a calculating gaze. Racine was a lovely woman, if a little flat–chested. Maybe that would work in her favor for Quinn. "I have to meet the same conditions, remember? It's taken care of. Just give Gage the money I gave you. Stop being such a cunt."

#

"So, are we good?" Racine asked. She tapped her long fingernail on the bar, lips pursed.

137

Gage gave her a good look up and down, but just could not see what anyone might find attractive about this banshee in Bebe. The woman practically hauled Gage away from the lunch table by the ear in her absurd and inexplicable fury.

"Yeah. We're good," Gage said as he finished counting out the wad of cash Racine handed him. It would not be 'good' if she'd done something stupid like stiff him. Then her dirty laundry would be aired out in front of everyone in the whole of Italy. Five thousand dollars cash was a strong motivator, however. So was another five thousand worth in precious powder. He didn't know where Racine got it, and felt it was safest not to ask.

"Good," she said, still circling him like a shark in the water. He frowned at her.

"What now?" he sighed. She smiled, bright white teeth hiding her forked tongue.

"You're not gay too, are you Gage?" she purred, coming up close to his face.

"Get away from me, Racine," he snarled, shoving her back. "No one is desperate enough to marry you. *No one.* I will happily suck someone else's cock before I let you come near me. Just like Quinn."

"What?" Racine growled between clenched teeth. "Are you telling me, he's *not* gay?"

"No, stupid, I'm telling you you're the kind of woman that makes men gay – the kind no man actually wants. Your twat's been used by everyone with a name, Racine. It's disgusting."

The slap that crashed across Gage's face brought stars to his vision. Her fake nails left scratches along his cheekbone. He snarled at her, but she was already walking away in a rage. This was not over.

#

Marjorie Lang watched her eldest son make obscene advances on yet another woman. His wife, Paige, sat with their daughter, pretending not to notice. It was a common sight to see among the elite. Marjorie had done it plenty of times. On the other side of the beautifully manicured lawn, her youngest son sat with his phone attached to his face. She'd seen him with Angel earlier, but only briefly.

Quinn remained absent, the whole castle whispering about why the couple was not at breakfast that morning. She needed to talk to Quinn to be sure he understood how important it was to have him *seen*. That was when she caught sight of the devil himself. Angel Rivera. She'd done her homework on him and his family. They were nothing. *Angel* was nothing. He worked for an Earth First lobbying company despite telling them he worked for a small law firm. His mother worked in custodial services at a high school in Fairfax, Virginia; stepfather was a retired police officer. There were an ungodly number of siblings, step-siblings, half-siblings. There was probably a bastard somewhere in there too, if she dug deep enough. He was good looking, though, and seemed to make Quinn happy. She supposed that had to be good enough. God knew Quinn wouldn't be able to find something better. Despite her husband's good intentions, Racine Fier was *not* of good stock.

"Oh, Angel!" Marjorie called to him, waving her hand. She had one of the passing staff refill her champagne flute and placed a smile on her face as Angel came to her with the 'work friend' who'd come with his sister. "You haven't seen Quinn, have you?"

"Everyday," Angel quipped back. The woman with him tried to hide a smile, but Marjorie saw it. She was too fat to hide anything beneath her cheap, generic clothes. Poor dear. Marjorie merely made a noise that could have been taken as a positive noise under the right circumstances.

"I meant recently, Angel. I need to talk to him," she clarified.

"He's napping. We had a long night," Angel replied. The audacity. She didn't need to know the details of their unfortunate relationship.

"I see. Well, sit, you and I can discuss it then. Is this your work friend? I don't think we've met."

"Yeah, this is Rachel Givens. Rachel, Marjorie Lang – Quinn's mom," he said with all the delicacy of a rhino in a China shop. So uncultured. Quinn could do so much better. She had half a mind to speak with Cameron D'Croix – her son was gay.

"Nice to meet you," Rachel said.

"I'm sure," Marjorie said. "I assume Quinn has gone over the terms of inheritance with you."

"Mrs. Lang –" Angel began, but she cut him off. She needed him to be comfortable.

"Oh, please, Angel, I don't need to feel *old*. Marjorie is fine."

"Right," he breathed out. "Uhm, I'm not marrying Quinn because of his money."

"I know," Marjorie intoned. She drained her champagne flute just thinking about her son being *intimate* with this man. It was disturbing. "But there's a problem that you should be aware of."

"A problem with…"

"The inheritance, sweetie, try to keep up," Marjorie said, setting the flute back down for it to be refilled. She sipped idly at the champagne as soon as there was more to sip, using it as a tool in her hands. "It wasn't an issue with our older two because, well, they're straight, but you simply don't have what it takes to fulfill the terms of that contract."

"I'm afraid I don't understand what you're getting at," Angel said. God, it was a good thing he was cute.

"A uterus, Angel. You don't have a uterus."

Rachel choked on her drink, dribbling it down her chubby chin. Poor girl. She'd be single forever.

"Last I checked, no, I did not have a uterus," Angel agreed. "I'm still not really sure why that matters....?"

"Because children are part of the contract, sweetheart. But don't worry, I've been talking to Larry about making an exception for adoption. After all, we adopted all of ours, right? Of course, you would need to move out of that tiny apartment. That's just not conducive to children at all..."

#

Angel felt his jaw hit the table. Everything else Marjorie Lang said came to him as 'blah blah blah blah'. She could not *possibly* be serious. But, of course, it made sense when he stopped to think for longer than a millisecond. If there weren't further conditions, the other two would have married and annulled as soon as the money hit the bank account – which was *exactly* what Angel and Quinn planned on doing until the previous night. Now it was… well, it was still a little up in the air, but *kids*? Angel didn't want children, not yet. Eventually, it might need to be a discussion, but the way Mrs. Lang was talking, they wanted an immediate turnaround.

Bella's kids ran across the lawn at that exact moment. All three were under five. Mackenzie was ten. They *were* immediate turnarounds.

He felt Rachel give his arm a squeeze beneath the table, bringing him back to the moment at hand.

"Mrs. Lang, could you give us a minute? I think Angel needs to go lie down."

"Are you feeling alright?" Mrs. Lang asked with all the concern of a rusted nail.

"D–dizzy," he stammered, surprising himself with that stutter. Shock could also induce a seizure.

"I just don't want him having another seizure," Rachel said, already pushing her chair back to haul him up to his feet. Angel went willingly, stammering apologies at Mrs. Lang even as he felt his breath begin to catch in his chest.

"Angel, look at me," Rachel commanded once they were safely tucked away from Marjorie

Lang's prying eyes. "Angel."

"Y–yeah. I'm looking. I'm..." he tried.

"No, you're not. Your eyes are closed. Open your eyes, Angel."

He forced himself to hold a breath, count to ten, and finally opened his eyes. Rachel looked up at him with pure adulation and concern in her big brown eyes. Seeing her worried about him made Angel's stomach knot, and that guilt he'd felt a few days ago return tenfold.

"Now breathe," she continued, holding his hands in hers. Angel took in a slow, deep breath and let it out, repeating the act a few times until he was calm again.

"We are so fucked, Rae," Angel sighed. "That was *not* mentioned when I agreed to this."

"I figured as much. Your lovely tan turned several shades of ashen back there," Rachel teased. "Worry about it later. You still need to get through the 'married' part, remember?"

"That's a done deal, though, Rae, I said I would," Angel answered without thinking. "Wait, that's not what I meant. I mean, no–"

"Stop," Rachel said, giving his hands a little squeeze. "We can talk later. There's too many ears here, ok? Just keep breathing for me, handsome. I don't need to explain why we're rushing you to a hospital to Quinn."

Angel snorted, pulling Rachel into his arms for a hug. It was in that moment, he realized how much he needed *her* in his life, too.

He was definitely fucked.

145

13

Angel walked through the halls of the castle the following morning. He was alone, for once. It seemed odd to do so. It was quiet and easy to lose himself in that silence. The days blurred together, and the noise was so close to intolerable he wanted to scream. He could see how easy it was to beat someone down like that. No one noticed it was even happening.

The entirety of the invited guests, minus a small handful, vacated the castle to play some very odd scavenger hunt throughout the vineyards that included grand prizes of cars, money, or pieces of coveted art. It wasn't anything Angel was interested in. Leti went to try to win a new car because hers was 'a piece of shit'. It worked, that was the important part, but she was having fun playing 'Rich and Crazy'. Angel would not take that from her.

It *was* nice to pretend for a little while, to have no worries and every wish catered to. When they weren't posing or smiling for everyone, the atmosphere was breathtaking, the food was absolutely divine, and the drinks exquisite. So, Angel took the time to enjoy himself and *breathe*. Plus, after the bomb Marjorie Lang dropped on him, he needed the break before discussing it with Quinn.

"Hey," Rachel said, coming up beside him as he overlooked the pool. Quinn's younger brother was lounging there like a lizard. Angel looked over at Rachel and smiled. "Wanna go for a swim?"

"Not right now. Just enjoying the peace, honestly."

Rachel snorted, nodding. "No kidding. It's the first morning I've woken up with just a normal hangover and not a screaming hangover."

Angel laughed at that. She wasn't wrong. The drinking was intense. He tried to keep it to a minimum for health reasons, but it was *good* wine.

"Seems weird to have you getting married," Rachel said. Angel looked at her, feeling all the guilt he'd been putting off hit him square in the chest. "Don't. I'm ok."

"Rachel, I–"

"It's fine, Angel. I said *if* we hadn't found

anyone else, remember?" Rachel said in a quiet voice full of understanding Angel did not deserve. He wanted so badly to kiss her, to convey his heart to her in that act, but knew that even in a mostly empty castle, there were too many eyes to see. She noticed the look he gave her. "Don't. Not here."

"I know," he said, looking down at his feet instead. "Maybe I'll just go nap. Haven't been sleeping too much."

She nodded and let him go. Angel did as he said, shuffling back to his palatial suite to soak in the tub for a while, then crawl into bed for a well–deserved nap. His head hurt and his body was angry at the break in routine. He tried to maintain it, to exercise and eat what he should, but that was hard to do with so many things scheduled around him.

When he woke, Quinn was back in the room, smiling at him from the chair nearby.

"What?" Angel asked in a groan with a half smile curling his lips.

"Is it weird that I enjoy watching you sleep?" Quinn asked. The smile on Angel's face broadened.

"No," Angel said, stretching slightly. The look Quinn gave him made Angel's stomach flip. Rachel had the same effect. He tried not to think too hard on what that meant. One thing at a time and the next step was the rehearsal dinner for his *wedding*.

#

"You ok?" Quinn asked during lunch when the guests returned from the scavenger hunt. "You look a little green."

"Yeah, I'm ok. Overwhelmed, I guess," Angel answered. "Do you even know any of these people?"

Quinn snorted, shaking his head. "Not really. They're all friends of my parents, I guess. I stopped paying attention around middle school."

"Quinn!" Mrs. Lang said waving them over to where Bella stood with a middle eastern man.

"Quinn, you remember Indra and this is his brother, Fariz," Mrs. Lang said proudly. "This is Angel, Quinn's beau to be."

"Nice to meet you," Angel said, extending his hand. Mrs. Lang gasped like it was a crime, but the man accepted it and shook it firmly, as did his brother.

"Have we met before?" Indra asked. Angel's eyes narrowed, but he smiled and shook his head.

"No, I don't think so."

"We have. In Washington. You handed me a pamphlet on the 'Evils of Oil Emissions on the

Planet'. That was you, yes?"

"Indra," Bella warned, already embarrassed. The man ignored his wife. Quinn looked decidedly terrified, but Angel was done with the lies. He had too much to deal with already, including but not limited to his growing feelings for Quinn, continued feelings for Rachel, and a nauseating sensation in his stomach at the prospect of dealing with these people for another forty–eight hours. So, he smiled and nodded. Quinn's dad loitered nearby, frowning.

"Yeah, that was probably me," Angel replied, rocking on his heels without shame. Indra laughed and nodded, pointing a finger at Angel.

"Your literature was inspiring," Indra admitted. Angel could not stop the look of surprise from hitting his face. "It sits in our research and development department as inspiration to find something better."

"Indra," Bella warned again.

"Congratulations to you two. I would love to have more discussions with you, Angel."

"Anytime," Angel smiled just as Leti joined him. He watched Indra walk off with Bella hissing in his ear until they reached the three children she was always screaming at. The man scooped them all up like cherished angels. So far, he was the only person among the Lang clan or their extended guests with any genuine emotion.

"And this is?" Fariz asked. Leti smiled while Quinn got pulled away to get an earful from his dad.

"Leti," Angel said. "My sister."

"Charmed," Fariz said, taking her hand with a kiss. "Does she deliver pamphlets too?"

"N–no," Angel said with a surprising stutter. "No … she.. uhm … she… sit… just… sit…"

"Angel?" Leti asked. He could not answer. "Can you get that chair? Rachel!"

He felt like he was floating, moving without direction until he was stationary again. He continued to make an attempt at speech, but it did not work. "Angel?"

"M'tired," Angel grumbled.

"Ok. Come on, *papi*, let's go lie down then, yeah?" Leti told him. Again, he moved without moving, floating weightless through time and space until feeling all of his muscles go lax and heavy sleep take him.

#

"Christ, Leti, why didn't you say anything!" Quinn hissed as he came into the room.

"He's fine, Quinn. Fariz helped us," Leti said with a gesture at Rachel.

"Acupuncture," Fariz answered. "He will be well soon enough."

"Thanks," Quinn said as he tucked Angel in. He let the girls stay with Angel before escorting Fariz back out with another thanks for his help. The noise outside was enough to give *Quinn* a seizure. He took one look at the loitering crowd and made his way to the bar where his siblings were at to get a stiff drink.

"Where's your beau, Q?" Willow slurred. It was barely one in the afternoon, but his younger sister was already drunk. He was surprised *he* was still sober after the hollering his father had done about Angel's 'embarrassing lie'. Larry Lang did not believe Angel had epilepsy *or* that he worked for a law firm. In fact, Quinn was pretty sure his father was beginning to suspect a lot of things.

"Sleeping. He's not feeling well."

Willow snorted. He had a vague recollection of his parents leaving for a 'trip' and coming back with a baby. The same happened with Gage, but Willow was the one he begged for them to return. She was as horrible of a child as she was an adult.

Willow swaggered around in a bikini and see-through wrap, her copper skin covered in some kind of glitter. Her long black hair was worked into a thick fishtail braid that fell down past her waist. She was gorgeous – for a woman – a model in Beverly Hills that had everything but happiness and a decent personality.

"Aww, poor baby. Can't handle all the glitz and glamor?"

"Christ, Will, are you drunk already?" Elliott asked as he shuffled by them to the bar. They both watched the man pour himself a tumbler full of bourbon and down it like a shot. Willow snorted. "Where's what's-his-face, Q?"

Quinn rolled his eyes. "Angel, Elliott. His name is Angel."

"You know I don't believe you two for a fucking second," Willow growled, her speech still slurred and nearly unintelligible. "Daddy doesn't either. You're just doing this shit for the money, like Elliott and Bells did. Shit, you'll probably get *more* money for pretending you're gay. Ass. Racine says the same thing. Have you even said hi to her? She's here, you know. She's so pissed. She'd be better than that fuck you're fucking."

"Stuff it, Willow!" Quinn barked.

Quinn saw Gage slither in at that point, throwing himself onto one of the leather chairs in the bar. Bella followed shortly thereafter, rubbing her temples. Like Elliott, Bella shuffled behind the bar and found the vodka. Everyone had their vices.

"It's fucking true, but everyone's *so* happy that Quinn gets his fairy-tale ending. A great guy he's *happy* with, all of mom's attention, and all of dad's money with incentives."

"Willow!" Elliott barked. Quinn blinked at them both.

"I hope he drowns," Willow hissed, stumbling away from the rest of her siblings. Quinn looked at Gage and Bella, both as confused as he, then to Elliott.

"Was she serious?"

"Q, I dunno. You know mom. She was telling Avery Schuster something about starting a fund so you and uhm..."

"Angel," Gage and Bella said in unison.

"Sure," Elliott dismissed. "So you two could adopt or get a surrogate when you're ready for kids."

"We were ready for kids?" Bella snorted. "It's part of the deal."

"What? Since when?" Apparently, Quinn had glossed over that part of his dad's rules.

"Always," his remaining siblings all said. Quinn didn't know how to react except to gape like a fish. Elliott gave him a good pat on the back, refilled his tumbler, and left.

"Fun times, right Q?" Gage said. The kid pulled a baggie of white powder out of his pocket and took a quick sniff. Bella tsked at him and walked off with her glass full of vodka, with a literal splash of cranberry juice. Quinn groaned, remembering that Angel had wanted to talk to him about something. Now Quinn knew what that something was.

He stayed hidden after that, reading in the room while Angel slept. He *looked* like an angel when he slept, peaceful and a lot less green than he was earlier.

"You're staring at me again," Angel grumbled from the bed without moving, eyes barely open. Quinn smiled, marking the spot in his book, and setting it aside.

"Can't help it?" Quinn replied, hoping he sounded cute. Angel snorted, which meant Quinn sounded like the loser he really was. "Feeling better?"

"Yeah. I had a seizure, didn't I?"

Quinn nodded. Angel rolled onto his back to look at Quinn. He was cuter when he was groggy. Quinn had to stamp down the desire to jump his bones.

"Stress. I told you my family was insane," Quinn said, forcing the flush to his face to go away. "Plus, there's different weather, you know? And different trees. Maybe kombucha works different out here."

"Maybe," Angel chuckled. "What time is it?"

"Four. We've got a while until dinner still. No rush. Want anything?"

"A sledgehammer for my head?" Angel chortled.

"Fresh out of sledgehammers, but I've got Tylenol and water if it's bad."

"It's bad," Angel grumbled. Angel *never* took meds. He only took what was necessary to manage his epilepsy, and vitamins that were so holistic and granola that it was a wonder he didn't chew moss in the raw and call it restorative. Quinn didn't argue, however, rifling through his bag to find the Tylenol, and grabbing a bottle of cold water from the tiny mini fridge in the room. He walked it over, really looking at the room around him for the first time.

It was quiet, insulated against most of the noise in the castle. The windows opened to a private balcony, tapestries hung on the wall, and crystal from the ceiling, but the rest of the décor was just so over-the-top it made Quinn sick. Everything was such a lavish display of opulence. Not for the first time since embarking on this obscene venture, he wondered if it was really worth it, especially given what Willow had said. He didn't realize that children were part of the deal. It had never been expressly stated. Both Elliott and Bella had children within the first year of being married.

Shit. That's how he makes sure they can't

divorce after the money is dished out, he thought as he handed Angel the water and Tylenol.

"Deep thinking?"

"Hm? Oh, no, just thinking about Willow and Gage. Will was drunk by one and Gage is back to snorting cocaine when our parents aren't around." Angel blinked at him. "I would like to remind you once more that *I'm* the normal one in this fucked up family."

"No shit..." Angel said, taking the requested meds and lying back on the bed. While the color had returned to Angel's face, the headache worried Quinn.

"Hey, have you been taking your meds?" Quinn asked, sitting beside Angel on the bed.

"Yeah," Angel answered without opening his eyes. "I'm fine, Q. The meds help manage, not eliminate. We've been doing a lot. They make me tired, and your family is a lot to take on."

"I warned you," Quinn chuckled. Angel smirked and blindly smacked Quinn's side. Quinn leaned down and kissed Angel's brow. "Get more sleep. I'll wake you before dinner."

#

Gage cracked his neck as he left the Groom's table. The tables were all laid out for the rehearsal dinner, exactly as it would be for the reception. The Groom's table sat at the head of the designated area and the rest spread out around the outdoor dance floor. Everything was outside to enjoy the summer weather. The drinks for dinner had already been poured, both Quinn and Angel's silver flutes stamped with 'Mr. & Mr. Lang'. Angel's name didn't matter. Gage felt bad for the guy. He seemed nice.

As he went back inside, Gage felt someone grab his arm and tug him hard into an alcove. He grunted when his back hit the limestone wall. His stomach soured when he saw Willow *and* Racine blocking him in.

"Is it done?" Willow hissed. Gage yanked his arm from her grasp.

"Yeah, it's done. I put a tiny bit in his coffee yesterday and there's a shit ton of it in his champagne now. Happy?" Gage snipped. Willow grinned like a wolf.

"Good boy," she purred, caressing his face. Gage jerked away from her.

"It better kill him, Gage," Racine added.

"Fuck off, Racine. No one said anything about killing him."

"*I* did," Racine snarled. "And *I* paid you!"

"You said dope him, you stupid ho bag. I did that. Get out of my way."

Gage tried to move, but Willow stopped him. "Plant it in his stuff. It needs to be believable."

"Why do you care, Willow?" Gage snorted. "*You're* not marrying Q."

Willow let her viperous grin shift to Racine before settling back on Gage. "It's entertaining. Plant it, then sit back to watch the shit show."

The smile on Willow's face made Gage shiver as he finally shoved away from the two scheming wenches, already regretting what he'd done.

#

Two hours later, Quinn and Angel were bombarded with requests to smile, to hug, to kiss, to hold hands, pose beside a cake that looked like it was encircled by diamonds, and make stupid faces to appease the people at the rehearsal dinner. Pictures immediately went up onto social media with tags for the wedding, and toasts were made for a happy future in wedded bliss. Quinn didn't even realize the wedding was happening the following day until he looked at a calendar. They just needed to make it through one more day.

The DJ played a raucous playlist, a mix of typical wedding songs and things that had Willow practically stripping. Their parents tried to get her to calm down or get Gage off his phone, while Bella hollered at her children and Elliott pretended to listen to his wife while checking out another woman, all with their daughter sitting beside them.

Quinn felt sick to his stomach. Angel *looked* sick to his stomach.

"Hi, *Quinn.*"

"*Dios mio, otra vez esta puta de mierda,*" Leti grumbled. Angel elbowed her. Quinn didn't know what she said, but it didn't sound nice.

Quinn froze. He knew the voice, felt the nails digging into his shoulder and barely refrained from wincing. He was aware of Angel looking up at the woman that dug her claws into him before standing to *his* full height.

"Hi. I don't think we've met," Angel said. "I'm Quinn's fiancé, Angel."

"I'm the one that should be sitting where you are," Racine said. Quinn groaned but remained frozen beneath the witch's grasp.

"Really? Did you ask him to marry you first? I might have missed that," Angel continued in a tone that was all honey filled with nettles. Racine didn't respond. She huffed and stomped off, screaming for her father. Angel stayed standing, then tapped Quinn's shoulder.

"Thanks," Quinn said.

"Stand up, c'mon. We're dancing."

"Are you kidding? I trampled you last time," Quinn said, only to find himself on the dance floor for a second attempt at dancing in public. Everyone watched it happen, watched *Angel* kiss

Quinn during a slow song, then slink away to the buffet for snacks and drink refills.

"Thanks," Quinn repeated quietly. Angel merely grinned half-heartedly at him. "You're looking green again." Gage joined them, filling a plate with tiny meatballs and cheese like the college dweeb he was.

"You ok?" Quinn asked Angel, while watching his brother load up on food.

Silence.

"Angel?"

"Dude, are you pissing yourself?" Quinn caught from Gage, looking down at his brother's crotch before realizing that his brother was speaking *to* someone. Quinn's eyes immediately went to Angel.

A steady stream of liquid puddled around the other man's left leg right before he collapsed to the floor, thrashing in a wild seizure.

"Angel! ELLIOTT!" Quinn hollered, immediately dropping beside his fiance to hold him so he didn't bite his tongue or cause more damage to himself. Elliott was a neuro-surgeon. No one moved. The music stopped while everyone stared without offering a single ounce of help. Gage merely gaped, taking slow steps back until Elliott shoved him out of the way.

Everyone else just watched like they'd reached the crescendo of the evening's entertainment. Quinn wanted to scream.

14

Bella offered Quinn some coffee from the machine in the hospital. It came in a Styrofoam cup and smelled like Vietnam-era coffee beans and tar. It tasted about the same, but Quinn needed to stay awake. The dinner guests had all gone back to their respective rooms with whispered gossip passing amongst their lips. Quinn tried to ignore what he heard, but the anger that built up was not an easy thing to ignore.

"Your leg is bouncing, Q," Bella said in a low, husky whisper that suited her better than the hollering screech she normally spoke with. She laid her hand gently on his knee, stilling the bounce. Leti and Rachel sat with him. Oddly enough, Fariz was there too, holding Leti's hand. That was something unexpected, and sure to race through the rumor mill as well.

"They think he's some kind of druggie," Quinn finally blurted, feeling tears welling in his eyes and his chest grow tight. "They think that's why he fell over like that."

"They're full of shit," Leti spat. Bella glowered at her, but Quinn just wallowed in grief.

"You know better than to listen to the ass hats mom and dad associate with," Bella reminded him. It helped some to know that Bella did not think of Angel in that light. They'd both seen what drugs could do to someone. Gage had been using since the kid started middle school and Willow was still kicking a habit, all things she came by legally. Elliott had been the worst. Elliott had nearly died in Bella's arms, with Quinn screaming for the neighbors to call someone. The fact that he *only* drank now was a blessing.

"Elliott will take care of him," Bella assured. Quinn nodded, trying not to bounce the other leg. He was terrified of losing Angel. The man had gone so pale and stiff, then liquified so suddenly. Quinn had never seen a seizure that bad. Normally any seizures Angel had were minor, things that had him staring off into space for too long, or batting away at things that didn't exist while his eyes blinked too fast. They didn't happen often. Angel was good about eating right, exercising, taking his meds and vitamins, getting enough vitamin D, all that crap. This was downright terrifying.

"Hey," Bella said, drawing Quinn's attention to her. Tears rolled down his face. "He'll be ok, Q."

"Will he?" Quinn squeaked out. Bella took his cup and set it down on the ground before wrapping her arm around him so he could cry into her shoulder. Angel meant everything to him.

"You really do love him, don't you?" Bella said, stroking his hair. It was then that Quinn realized literally *no one* in his family believed that until that exact moment. They thought it was a ruse to get money like Bella and Elliott had done. The realization made him cry harder.

"So much, Bells. I don't know what I'll do if he's not ok," Quinn sobbed, acutely aware of *Rachel* watching him like his family did. None of the Lang children were particularly close. They didn't call each other like Angel did with his siblings. Quinn barely remembered to send Christmas cards and couldn't tell anyone their birthdays to save his life. They lived the lives their parents dictated and loathed every second of it. "Why do you and Elliott follow dad's rules, Bells? For what?"

"Same reason you're marrying Angel," Bella answered, still stroking his hair. Quinn sat up and looked at his sister. "The money. It's what's expected, Q."

"That isn't why I'm marrying Angel," Quinn said, meaning it in every fiber of his being. "This is my fault. I shouldn't have brought him here and put him under so much stress or pressure. I don't even know why I let them talk me into it. I don't care about money, Bella, I care about Angel!"

She nodded, shushing him a little as she placed his head back on her shoulder. She pretended to understand, to care. None of them understood, however, because all of them followed the same horrid pattern their parents built for them. Things were expected of them. They had to put on certain appearances. Quinn was done with it. He'd find a way to give Angel's family what they needed, but he was done.

"Quinn," Elliott said, making Quinn jump. Part of him thought his brother had heard his thoughts, but really, he was just too jumpy, too worried. Their dad stood there too, already walking to Elliott before Quinn could even stand up. "I'd like to talk to Quinn alone, dad."

"I don't think that's necessary," Larry Lang argued.

"I do," Elliott said, standing his ground. Within these walls, he wasn't anyone's son. He was a doctor, even in a foreign hospital. They'd requested that Elliott treat Angel. Their father did not appreciate being left out of the conversation.

Leti and Rachel stood too, but remained where they were.

"Remember who pays your mortgage," Larry hissed, and stepped away. Quinn watched him while Elliott took him aside.

"How is he?" Quinn asked as soon as Elliott tugged him into a corner away from the elder Lang. "Is he ok?"

"Sedated," Elliott cut in, looking far too serious for someone that should be the bearer of good news.

"Sedated? Why?"

"Q, what do you know about Angel's drug problem?"

"What drug problem? He doesn't have a drug problem," Quinn replied, suddenly defensive and angry. Elliott sighed. "Elliott, what are you talking about?"

"There was a lot of cocaine in his system, Quinn. He's lucky he's still alive. He's sedated because the seizures haven't stopped yet."

"What?" Quinn breathed out. He felt like his world was crashing in on him. Elliott had to be wrong. That was the only rational explanation. "No. You're wrong. He doesn't... he wouldn't... run the test again."

"I did," Elliott reported sadly. "You really didn't know about his drug habit?"

"He doesn't have one!" Quinn barked. "For fuck's sake, he's a goddamned vegetarian, Elliott! He takes his meds and recycles. He's a fucking lobbyist for climate change, for Christ's sake, not a fucking junkie!"

"Wow, really?" Willow giggled, the entire waiting room looking at him now. "How lame. Racey is going to *love* this."

"Fuck you, Will," Quinn barked, scrubbing at his face. He looked at the members of his family, all sitting there, all waiting. They were all in various states of interest, using Quinn's misery as their personal entertainment. "Did you do this? You're the one that wanted him to drown!"

"Quinn!" his mother screeched, appalled that he would make such an accusation. Except all of his siblings heard her and not a single one of them backed him up.

"Quinn, what the hell is going on?" his father asked. Quinn wanted to hit the man as hard as he possibly could and watch the blood trickle from his nose just to knock him off his high horse. "You know my rules."

"Fuck your rules," Quinn hissed. "I don't *care* about your rules! I *care* about my friend!"

"Friend?" Willow smirked. "Don't know too many engaged couples that refer to each other as 'friends'."

"Run the test again," Quinn said as he shouldered past Elliott. His vision blurred as tears streamed down his face and he growled at his brother when Elliott tried to tell him he was not allowed where Angel was. Quinn ignored him, ignored the other hospital staff hollering at him in Italian, and easily found the room, stopping short at the door.

Tubes and wires covered Angel. He had one that breathed for him, an IV line, EKG monitors, and several other things that Quinn couldn't place. There was no color to the Hispanic man, no movement save for the tiniest twitch of his finger that was recorded on one of the monitors.

"Dammit, Quinn, I told you, you can't be back here," Elliott said, finally catching up. Quinn didn't move. He could smell the antiseptic stench of everything Angel was surrounded by. The heart monitor seemed too slow, too quiet, while Quinn's own heart beat so loud he thought he might pass out. Maybe he did. The next time he remembered blinking, he was back at the castle with Bella and Mackenzie while Leti and Rachel stayed with Angel.

"Uncle Quinn, what's this?" Mackenzie asked as she moved some of the bags aside. White powder spilled out of a side pocket in Angel's bag. Bella noticed it, too.

"Do me a favor, Mackie, can you go make sure your heathen cousins are still asleep? I thought I just heard Juda."

Mackenzie nodded, setting the bag back down. Quinn couldn't move. His feet had rooted themselves to the carpet and all of him trembled. He was aware of Bella saying something to him, but not what it was until Bella smacked him sharply across the face.

"Ow! What was that for!"

"To get your shit together! Dad *cannot* find this, or it is over for you! He'll make you marry Racine," Bella hissed.

"But this... why would he do this?"

"Ask him later, cover it up now," Bella said. That was their existence: cover it up, lie, pretend. If no one saw it, then it wasn't real. But there it was — a sprinkling of white powder lining the side pocket of Angel's bag. Quinn helped his sister clean it all up, put Angel's bag up out of view, and tried to sleep. He thought about calling Rachel, about taking a walk, or drowning *himself* in the pool, but ultimately just stayed on the bed until the sun came up.

Quinn went back to the hospital after that to relieve the girls, skipping breakfast and pointedly ignoring eye contact with Bella. His father came in, grumbling something about trying to pull some trick to get money, about being a disgrace and a bunch of other things that Quinn didn't really hear. He felt the doubt sour his stomach, the what-ifs that made him really wonder if he knew Angel as well as he believed. He knew Angel had not been feeling well that day. Maybe something happened to trigger his seizures. Someone could have spiked his punch or something. Angel would tell him that things like that didn't happen in real life, only crazy romance movies. Except, Quinn's life was one big pathetic romance movie.

He sat in Angel's room so long that his legs went numb, curled up beneath him. Bella stopped by a few times and Elliott checked on them both. Rachel and Leti sat with him for long periods of time, breaking only to use the restroom or to eat. No matter what anyone said or did, Quinn never moved. He didn't eat, barely drank anything, and barely slept, nodding off from time to time when exhaustion was too much for him to fight. He felt raw, inside and out.

When Quinn finally slept longer than thirty minutes, he woke with a crick in his neck, a killer headache, and his niece's sweet voice talking softly to someone.

"... to stay."

"I don't think that's such a good idea anymore, kiddo."

"Maybe I can come visit?"

"Sure, I'd like that," Angel croaked. He could barely speak, but Mackenzie was a good conversationalist, so he put in the effort for her. He'd seen Quinn first, then Mackenzie who was playing her Switch on the floor when Angel's eyes finally acquiesced cooperation. It became clear very quickly that something terrible had happened. The monitors and cloud-stuffed feeling in his head told him that without having to look at the big bold letters right outside his room that read 'Intensive Care' in Italian. He didn't even read Italian, but it was close enough to Spanish for him to figure it out. Unfortunately, Mackenzie only knew that he'd collapsed, and it made everyone mad.

"Angel?" Quinn said, moving from his chair slowly, as if afraid to approach. Mackenzie moved back, picking up her Switch so she could take the chair Quinn had been in instead.

"Mackenzie said I 'died or something'," Angel said, trying to put some levity into his words. By the sheen in Quinn's eyes, he either hit too close to the truth or failed miserably.

"Jesus, Angel," Quinn breathed, dropping heavily to the edge of the bed. He took Angel's hand in his, giving it a squeeze. "I can't..."

"I'm fine," Angel assured as Quinn nearly folded in half to place his head on Angel's chest. "Q?"

"You scared the shit out of me. I don't even know what's happening right now, Angel but–"

"What even happened?" Angel interrupted. Quinn blanched.

"Angel, you OD'd." There was hesitation on Quinn's face before he continued. "Bella and I took care of it. Why didn't you tell me? I would have found a way to get you help or–"

"Wait, hang on. I OD'd? On *what*?"

"Cocaine," Quinn whispered sadly. "Angel–"

"Move," Angel growled. Quinn blinked, watching as Angel shoved himself up on the bed, looking at all the things attached to him with disdain.

"Where are you going?" Quinn asked.

"Home, dammit. I'm going home. I can't believe you'd think for one *second* that I'd do shit like that! Have you gone mental! Did you even bother to ask Leti?! Or Rachel?!"

Mackenzie watched them, her eyes big and curious, ears absorbing everything.

"Angel, Bella and I found it in your bag," Quinn hissed. Angel stopped moving. Rage filled his vision. The ringing in his ears turned into a high–

pitched scream that made his breath catch in his chest. No, he really couldn't breathe. It was too hard, brought him too much effort.

"Angel! Look at me! Angel!"

"...home... go home...." Angel heard himself repeat, feeling oddly detached from himself even as he looked up at Quinn from the floor.

15

Angel checked himself out of the hospital the following morning and was on a plane with Leti and Rachel before the day's end. Quinn sat in the bridal suite staring at the spot where Angel *should* have been sleeping and tried not to cry. He'd packed his things too and called a cab to take him to the airport. Angel hadn't even gotten his bag, just left without another word spoken.

"Son?"

Quinn did not respond to his father's voice. He sat there in numb silence.

"Quinn, look, I spoke to Maxey Fier and–"

"I swear to God if you finish that sentence, you will be *burying me* by the end of the week!" Quinn growled, tears welling in his eyes. "Are you fucking kidding me! The man I *love* is gone, dad!

Gone! He left because ... because I'm a piece of shit and believed *you fucking twats* over the man I've lived with and loved for six years. Angel would *never...* I'm going home. *Home* to DC and I am going to *beg* at his feet for forgiveness because I will *not* go to my grave with Angel thinking I believed any of your fucking lies."

"Now, hang on, I haven't done anything but try to give you and your siblings the best life possible. I have conditions for it and Angel broke it. So did you. You're not even gay."

"ARE YOU EVEN LISTENING TO ME!" Quinn roared. "*LOVE,* dad. I *LOVE* Angel Rivera with every fucking fiber of my being, and you RUINED IT! Why couldn't you and mom just leave me alone! Why did you have to stop by! I don't want your goddamned money. I don't want anymore of your condition–laden handouts! I want Angel, dad. Do you even know what that's like?! You know what, forget it."

Quinn grabbed his bag and Angel's, awkwardly hauling them to the foyer with tears streaming down his face while his father hollered behind him. He would be disowned, he was overreacting, what would everyone think? Quinn didn't care what anyone but Angel thought, and Angel believed that Quinn thought he was a drug addict.

The only thing that mattered now was making things right.

#

Angel spent three days in the hospital once he got home from Italy. In fact, he was taken off the plane on a stretcher and immediately transported by ambulance to INOVA Fairfax Hospital, where his doctors were located. Rachel and Leti stayed with him the first day, with the rest of his family filling in the time with brief visits and prayers. He was vaguely aware of them, in and out of consciousness for the first day and a half, then allowed to leave, finally, when he went more than five hours without a seizure.

He didn't bother going to his apartment. He didn't want to be there, or near anything that reminded him of Quinn. Rachel let him stay with her, let him share her bed just to sleep and recover, to be held without scrutiny. Angel's chest hurt, his head felt detached from the rest of his body. Rachel said it was lingering effects of whatever drug was in him. Angel wasn't so sure.

It was Angel's *heart* that hurt the most.

"Hey, you hungry?" Rachel asked from the bedroom door. Angel merely shook his head, feeling numb to the world. "Baby, you need to eat something. You're just going to make yourself worse if you don't."

"I'm not hungry, Rae," Angel sighed. He could hear the croak in his own voice and mentally sighed again. He didn't want to do much of anything lately. Initially, Angel believed it was just his poor state of health, but he knew that was not the only reason.

He missed Quinn.

The idiot broke his heart and would not stop calling, or stopping by, or sending texts. Angel ignored all of them. Thinking of Quinn made that pain in his chest come back tenfold.

"Angel," Rachel said, sitting beside him. "Baby, please eat something. Just some soup? Something light?"

Angel simply looked up at the woman that held a piece of his heart; the piece that wasn't broken. He didn't want food. He wanted Rachel. She made a noise of surprise when he pulled her into a kiss, but didn't push him away. He needed to taste and touch her, wanting the comfort of her round body like any normal human being might want the comfort of a warm blanket on a cold winter day. She was his warmth.

It did not take long for their kiss to become impassioned, or for her clothing to fall away beside the bed. His clothing followed. The sheets were soft against his bare skin, the blankets a soothing weight on his legs. Rachel straddled him, sliding over his shaft as if re-sheathing a long-lost sword. Angel groaned into the kiss, holding her hips lightly. She did all the work, hips moving along his, grinding against him.

Angel kissed her for a while, enjoying the feel of her, then let her catch a breath as he buried his face in her breasts. He suckled each one, drawing out little whimpers of joy as he sought comfort within her.

"Oh God, Angel.." she breathed as they made love, pleasuring each other until they were both drawing ragged breaths, kissing and touching and screaming with pleasure. They stayed that way after, as if Rachel knew that Angel needed the intimacy to help heal him.

"I love you," she said to him, stroking his hair as he rested against her shoulder. He didn't have it in him to reply with anything but hot tears that slid down his face.

#

"Quinn came by again," Rachel said a couple weeks later.

Angel remained silent, still feeling like the underside of a chewed shoe. His appetite had been for shit since returning to DC, and he'd had two more seizures that freaked the hell out of Rachel. Quinn had come by every single day since his return, but Angel didn't want to see him, so

Rachel kept turning him away — God bless her.

"Angel, you're going to have to talk to him eventually."

Maybe God didn't have to bless her...

"I don't want to," Angel croaked. Rachel came to sit by him, shifting their positions so his head could rest in her lap. She ran fingers through his hair, idly braiding it or just carding fingers. It felt good, helped him to relax. Her home smelled like apple-cinnamon wall plugins and the ziti they'd just eaten for dinner. Not that he'd eaten much of it. What mattered most was how *normal* everything was. Her couch came from the thrift store. Her TV was a little crooked on the wall because she put it up with the help of one of her girlfriends who was so short Rachel called her Pixie Trish. There was no one to impress, no one to pretend for, no one to lie to.

"Angel?" Rachel asked. Angel raised his eyebrows by way of response. "Sweetie, you're crying."

Angel's eyes snapped open. His vision blurred. He hadn't even realized it. He felt the tightness in his chest and stomach, but he'd felt like that for the last few weeks. Then Rachel's doorbell rang.

"He's nothing if not punctual," Rachel sighed. Angel scrubbed frantically at his face.

"What do I tell him?"

"The same, I don't want to see him."

Rachel nodded, leaving him on the couch while she went to answer the door. Angel could hear the rain against the roof now, each drop ricocheting off the balcony rails.

"Quinn, you really need to stop–"

"Please," Quinn cut her off. "Please. I just need to say one thing and I swear I'll never come back. Please."

The door didn't close. Angel didn't move, staying perfectly still with his back to Quinn. He could *feel* the other man's presence. It made his spine tingle uncomfortably.

"I'm sorry," Quinn started, sounding as if he'd run through the rain with how often he sniffled. "I'm so, so sorry. There is nothing I can ever say that will change how horribly I betrayed you. For what it might be worth, I would've bought any cake you wanted for our wedding, even if it was just a pound cake from the store because it's what *you* wanted. I should have told them that day. I knew better, but I still let my family force my thoughts, and push away the one person I love with all my being; let them *hurt* you. I shouldn't have. I should have put a stop to it before it even started and... I know I'll never get you back and that hurts more than I can explain, but you needed to know that I'm an asshole and you deserve better."

Silence.

Angel didn't move or breathe until Rachel came to sit beside him again. He was frozen, with tumultuous thoughts and emotions. Rachel waited, tucking hair behind his ear, or holding his hand until the tears he'd scrubbed away returned.

"Let it out, baby," she said softly, adding the endearment in a way that shifted their entire dynamic. He didn't want things to change so much.

That was the crux of it.

Everything changed. His relationship with Quinn was destroyed. His relationship with Rachel was... something. Even Leti was treating him differently. The comforts that he leaned upon so heavily were crumbling out from beneath him, leaving him grasping at air so he wouldn't fall over.

He looked at Rachel, wanting to say something to her, but she closed the space between him and kissed him sweetly. His heart exploded with joy and pain and desperation he could not explain. He brought his hand to her face to hold her to him, but she pushed away, already knowing more than he did.

"Go," she whispered. "Go talk to him."

"Rachel, I–"

"I'm not going anywhere, Angel. We're growing old together, remember?" she said, pressing her brow to his. "Go talk to him. I'll still be here. I promise."

"I don't know what to tell him," Angel finally admitted. His stomach was a riot of knots and violent grumbles that made him nauseous. Rachel merely smiled, caressing his face.

"Well, if you look at him and feel all those knots in your stomach release, then let it happen. If not, come back to me. I'll be here no matter what."

"I love you," Angel said. It was not the first time he'd said those words to her. She'd said them to him plenty of times. He knew they loved each other in a way that went beyond mere friendship or passive lovers. She smiled at him and kissed the tip of his nose.

"I love you too. Go on."

In the grand scheme of things, Rachel did not live very far from where Angel used to reside. *Used to.* He didn't like how that sounded, even if it was only in his head. The Metro stop to Rachel's place was two stops down from where Angel might normally get off for Rock Creek. It was why he didn't mind keeping Rachel safe or meeting her on the way to and from work. He could Metro or take the bus, but he needed the time to think, to breathe, so he walked in the rain, feeling the cool sting on his face and neck in stark contrast to the summer humidity.

It felt good to walk in the rain, to let the water cleanse him of the negativity that lingered, the doubt that clouded his thoughts, and the fury that filled his heart. His steps slowed, the rain saturating all of him until he stood beneath the torrent of water with his face turned up to the sky. He became aware of his breathing, slowed his heart rate, and relaxed his muscles. He couldn't go into this with clouded emotions. And, while he was a mess of confusion and wild feelings, he needed to give Quinn a chance to explain, to hear *Angel's* side of things.

The rest of the walk back to the apartment in Rock Creek was done with a silent mantra to calm him until he walked up the steps instead of using the elevator, standing in front of the apartment door like a wet rag. Even then, Angel struggled to lift his arm to knock, shivering instead as if it were ten degrees outside rather than eighty.

Finally, he gathered his courage and knocked.

"... dude, I already put the tip on the damn — Angel," Quinn said, coming up short at the door as if hitting an invisible wall. Angel looked at Quinn, looked at how rucked up he looked. He hadn't shaved, had bags under his eyes, and looked like he'd been wearing the same clothes all week long.

He probably had, knowing Quinn. "Uhm... w–what are you doing here?"

The question seemed a little ridiculous. All of Angel's furniture was still *in* the apartment. Hell, all his *clothes* were in the apartment. He'd gone shopping so he would have clothes at Rachel's house rather than risk running into Quinn.

"All my stuff is still here," Angel said. It was not what he'd planned on saying, but that's what came out. Quinn's face immediately fell, eyes looking down to the floor as he nodded.

"Right. Of course. Uhm. Do you want me to help you pack or ..."

"No," Angel said. He didn't want to pack. The knots that were in his stomach vanished in the rain and did not return, even while he stood out in the hall making a puddle. Quinn nodded again, swallowing down whatever lump Angel knew was in his throat, and stepped aside.

"I'll... uhm... I'll just sit over–"

"I love you, I think," Angel blurted. It was also *not* what he'd intended on saying; especially the 'I think' part. He knew he'd already told Quinn he loved him but it seemed different now, more... real. "Uhm.. it's weird. I shouldn't. You're an ass, but I don't like that you're not there for breakfast. I don't like watching football alone with an attack Chihuahua. I *wanted* to marry you. But... I can handle them trying to off me. It would figure, you know? They're crazy. But you… Quinn, you've been my practical shadow since college and you just… *believed* them. That hurt. Anyway, I just… figured you should know that."

Silence.

Angel nodded, sniffed, and looked at the new puddle he was making on their favorite rug.

"Ok," Quinn finally said. "So… now what?"

Angel shrugged and huffed a little, still trembling from being wet and the sudden blast of AC filling the hall and apartment. Quinn finally noticed.

"Did you *walk* here?"

"It's raining."

"I know. I… Angel, does *Rachel* know how you feel? I mean, really know, not just what she gleaned in Italy?"

Angel nodded, biting his lip to get control of the tremors. Silence fell between them again, putting all the background noises into sharp focus.

Angel heard the ticking of the clock mounted on the wall like a gong in his mind. The AC unit made a whirling noise that rattled one of the grates near the kitchen. There was the constant bubbling noise from the fish tank near the window and the creaks and groans of their neighbors moving through their homes on either side of

Angel and Quinn's apartment.

"...gel? Hey. Look at me."

Angel blinked and suddenly felt dizzy.

"Come on. Come sit down," Quinn said, guiding him to the couch. Angel nodded, holding on to Quinn to steady his steps. He let Quinn remove his sopping wet clothes and wrap him in a warm blanket while his mind continued to zone in and out.

"Angel, are you–"

"Fine," Angel cut in. "Sit down."

Quinn complied, staring with concern and fear on his face. Angel took a few deep breaths, then finally looked at Quinn. He wanted to say more, to explain how he was feeling and the confusion that came with it. Instead, he leaned in and kissed Quinn deep and long, holding him close until he *had* to draw breath.

"Can we start over?" Angel said against Quinn's lips. "Can we pretend you're still the tubby kid from college and just a basement troll secretly in love with his roommate and I'm ... apparently confused but open to new things like mind–blowing sex with my fake fiancé? Can we do that?"

Quinn snorted a dry, nervous laugh but nodded. "Yeah. Yeah, we can do that."

"Good," Angel said while nodding, leaning in to kiss Quinn again, this time with intensified passion and bruising need, opening the blanket to pull Quinn in.

16

Gage Lang stood at the far end of the hall leading to his father's study. The man's voice carried across the mahogany floors of their obscenely large home. Gage rarely walked over to where the study was because his room was in the opposite wing. He was the only one of his siblings still living in the house, and that was only when he was not at school. Any chance he got, he was somewhere else.

He wiggled his fingers against sweaty palms and forced his feet to move, taking one step, then another until he was standing at the door to the study. It was always open, giving the illusion that all were welcome. Gage never made that assumption. Or rather, he was never allowed to. Quinn was the one to warn him against going into their father's study; Quinn was the one to help him kick his drug habit once already; Quinn was the one that sent him birthday cards every year. Granted, they came in March instead of May, but the day was right. It was an attempt that no one else made, parents included.

He stood for a few seconds longer before knocking on the door frame. Larry Lang looked up from his desk, pen in hand, and set it down.

"Something wrong, Gage?"

Gage's voice seized in his throat.

"Son, I don't have time for nonsense," his father said, going back to the paper on his desk. Gage stepped forward enough to glance at it, easily reading the words upside down. It was a legal document removing Quinn from the family.

"I drugged Angel," Gage blurted. The pen stopped again. "Will and Racine talked me into it. So you'd make Q marry Racine."

"I'm not interested in practical jokes, Gage."

"I'm not joking," Gage said, tossing the baggie he normally kept in his pocket onto his father's desk. White powder spilled across the cursed paper. "It's mine. I started using again when I got to Stanford."

"Again? Is this some kind of sick game?"

"No," Gage said, shaking his head. "Quinn helped me get clean. He didn't tell anyone because... because he knew you'd be pissed.

Neither of you ever cared to check."

"Your mother and I have rules, son," his father started, but Gage shook his head and cut him off.

"No, *you* have rules. You have so many fucking rules, it's sick! You treat us all like pedigree dogs instead of kids! All of us! And every single one of us is so fucked up inside we run to the nearest bottle or pill to make it go away. Everyone but Quinn. He plays video games instead. And I won't lie for Racine Fucking Fier. She's a witch on wedges. Quinn deserves better than that. He *deserves* to be happy. We all do. No matter what your fucking rules say."

Gage walked out of the study, forcing himself to ignore the clarion call of his father's voice demanding he return and explain himself. He was almost twenty; he didn't need to explain himself to anyone. He'd told his dad. Next, was apologizing to Quinn. That took a little more planning because the idiot lived across the country. He was the only one that got away before their dad's insane rules came crashing down on his head. Well, almost, anyway.

The family's driver was waiting for him by the time Gage reached the front door. He got in the back and absently reached for the baggie that was no longer in his pocket.

"Fuck," he groaned. It was going to be a very long flight to DC.

#

Angel listened to his sister turn into a puddle of mush while talking to Fariz Amad during their family's weekend BBQ. They were probably the most unlikely couple in all of creation, yet he'd heard her giggle four times in as many minutes; *giggle*. At least one good thing came out of all the insanity in Italy.

The thought made him glance over to where Rachel sat with Angel's other sister, Sylvia, and her two kids, coloring with 'magic' markers. He brought Rachel to his family's gatherings now, right along with Quinn. She was the reason his *abuelita* asked about great-grandchildren anytime he came to visit. Neither of them had the heart to tell the old woman that Rachel could not have children. In fact, the thought had crossed Angel's mind more than once to adopt, especially after seeing how Quinn's family royally fucked up how such a thing was *supposed* to work.

"Do you think Quinn got lost again?" Angel's mother asked, as she came up beside him with a giant platter of freshly roasted corn, popping his thought bubble and replacing it with a growling stomach instead. They'd sent Quinn out for more ice and drinks.

"Probably," Angel chuckled. They'd all heard what happened, heard about the fallout and slow-burning make-up between Angel and Quinn. They were taking it slow, truly deciding on how they each felt and where Rachel fit into everything. Angel made it very clear to both of them that he would not, and could not, continue on without *both of them* in his life, nor would he lie to either of them. He loved them both, even if that felt weird. Not wrong, just weird.

That revelation lifted the weight of guilt he'd been carrying around in Italy. No one said you *had* to love only *one* person for all of eternity. In fact, family often proved that logic to be incorrect. Parents did not love their children more or less than the other when there was more than one child. The same logic could be placed on partners as well. He told Leti and his mom about his feelings, letting everything else fall into place on its own.

"Help! Heeeelp!" Quinn called from the door. Angel looked at his mom and sighed when she wrinkled her nose and clucked out a little laugh. He wiped his hands and walked out to where Quinn stood, overloaded with cases of water and soda.

"You could've gone for more than one trip, Q!" Angel admonished, relieving his boyfriend of the burden he carried; or, part of it at least.

"I had it," Q argued. "Mostly."

They enjoyed the day with Angel's family, cooking out and floating along their brand new pool. His parents were very proud of that addition, eager to host *everything* from lunch to parties as a result of their hard work. The evening was loud and raucous, but full of acceptance and genuine love. It was where Angel belonged.

He dozed in the back seat of Rachel's car on the way home, worn out by the day's events. It was the kind of exhaustion he yearned for; the kind earned from a good life lived.

"You coming up tonight?" Quinn asked Rachel, making Angel grin with his eyes still closed. Quinn spent almost two weeks *certain* Angel was going to ditch him again and run off with Rachel. It was nice to see him accepting his place beside her as an equal now.

"No, I can't. I've gotta go let Juju out of her kennel cuz I've been gone all day," Rachel sighed.

"Juju? Your creepy cute dog's name is Juju?"

"She's not creepy! Yeah, her name is Juju," Rachel chortled.

"That's the name of my succulent..." Quinn said, reaching around to gently shake Angel awake.

"See, you have more in common than you

think," Angel mumbled, eyes still closed.

"You're supposed to be asleep," Quinn said. Angel merely smiled. He kissed Rachel's cheek from the back seat and promised to call in the morning before walking up to the apartment with Quinn's hand in his.

Both men's steps slowed when they saw what awaited them in the hall.

"Gage?" Quinn squeaked. "What are you doing here?"

The kid looked rough. His hair was a mess, and his skin was looking a little sallow. Stubble grew on his chin and it looked like he spent the last few days in the same clothes.

"Hey, bro," Gage slurred in a weak croak. Any and all exhaustion immediately evaporated from Angel. Quinn too, for that matter. He let Angel's hand go so he could squat in front of his brother.

"Gage, how high are you?" he asked, feeling the kid's brow. Angel frowned at that, remembering how easily Quinn believed he'd turned to drugs. It was like a default setting to assume such things for Quinn. "Gage!"

"M'not... I dumped it all on dad's desk," the kid replied.

"You what?!"

"Shhhhhhhh," Gage said, batting Quinn

down. "Not so loud, jeez. My head hurts. And m'hungry. Got any food?"

"Ok, we can discuss this inside," Angel cut in, helping Quinn get Gage to his feet even as he unlocked the door. "C'mon. In."

Gage complied, stumbling through the door, tripping on the rug at the same spot Quinn always tripped on, before collapsing on the couch. Angel's mom had packed them enough leftovers to last the entire week, but Rachel kept them, so Angel went to dig through their fridge and pantry, finding a fresh box of donuts first. It seemed a little cliche, but it was quick and required no cooking, so Angel grabbed them.

"Here," he said, handing Gage the box.

"Those are mine," Quinn whined. Angel threw him a frown while Gage dug into the box like a man starved. They watched him in silence for a few minutes, waiting until the kid had eaten half the box. Angel retrieved some water for him too, that was consumed just as quickly.

"You're going to make yourself sick," Angel commented in slight disgust. Gage shrugged.

"Already am. Detoxing sucks. I got lost getting here and ended up... I dunno. But I got more and then got lost again. I didn't write your address down right. I had it as Rock Park. No one knew what I was talking about."

"Gage, how long have you been here?" Quinn asked. Again, the kid shrugged.

"Week, maybe. I dunno. I passed out for part of it."

Angel and Quinn shared a worried look between each other, then waited for Gage to finish the box of donuts and drink more water than a camel in the desert. Angel became hyperaware of the sounds in his apartment again, stamping down the worry and tension by digging his fingernails into the palms of his hands. He'd never had such a dreadful feeling before. It bothered him.

"Hey, are you ok? Do you need to sit down?" Quinn asked quietly, suddenly in Angel's face. Angel blinked, all the sound rushing back to his ears but nodded, forcing himself to take slow breaths.

"I'm fine. Help your brother."

"I'm good, dude, just tired. I did all the puking yesterday," Gage said, as if he had experience with detoxing. Given what Angel knew about Quinn's family, he probably did.

"Gage, what are you doing here? Do mom and dad know you're here?"

Gage shook his head, as he leaned over onto the couch.

"Just wanted t'say m'sorry," Gage muttered, already falling asleep in his dirty clothes.

"Sorry for what? Gage?" Quinn asked, but Gage was already out like a light. Quinn looked up at Angel, worry on his face.

#

Elliott Lang sat with his head on the back of the leather sofa that smelled new even after forty years of existence. Longer if he knew his parents, but Elliott was only forty. Paige sat beside him, prim and proper, back straight and lips pursed in disapproval at what she was being subjected to. Elliot's father ranted and railed about the disgrace that was befalling the family, dragging their good name through mud, blah, blah, blah. He'd even called Bella and Indra, telling them both they were needed for a 'family discussion'.

They weren't a family.

They were people that shared the same last name and little more. Elliott and Paige barely spoke. When they did, it was only to argue with each other. Elliott liked women and a good drink. Paige didn't like anything. She'd married him for his money. Mackenzie sat on the floor between them, the product of their contractual obligation to procreate. They'd only done it enough for Paige to get pregnant and never touched each other again.

Bella lucked out with Indra. He seemed nice and was gone most of the time. Clearly, they fucked enough when he was around for them to have *three* snotty brats around their ankles, none of whom were present. They were smarter than Elliott and Paige, leaving their brood with the nanny. Willow and Gage didn't even bother to show. The only one not mentioned once thus far was–

"– – Quinn's fiance. Now I want answers, dammit!" Larry Lang growled, drawing Elliott's attention up for the first time since the tirade began.

"I thought they broke up. It's after his birthday, he didn't go through with the contract," Elliott said.

"God, Elliott, pay attention," Paige sighed, embarrassed for both of them.

"Where *is* Gage, dad?" Bella said, throwing a glare at Paige. No one liked the woman.

"That's what I'd like to know! He left after throwing a bag of cocaine on my desk and claimed *he* poisoned Angel!"

"That's absurd, Larry. Gage doesn't do drugs," Marjorie said. Elliott glowered at her.

"Are you for real?" he dared.

"Elliott!" Paige hissed. He silenced himself immediately and just glared at his wife.

"Uncle Quinn and Aunt Bella flushed the white powder they found down the toilet,"

Mackenzie said without looking up from her stupid game. "Angel didn't do it, though. I heard Aunt Willow telling Uncle Gage he *had* to do it. I like Angel. He's nice. He makes Uncle Quinn happy."

Silence.

The sound of Mackenzie's game echoed into the high ceiling.

"Mackie, why would you say something like that?" Paige whispered, face red and voice trembling with barely contained rage. Mackenzie did not look up from her game, shrugging.

"Uncle Quinn took me to get ice cream. All he talked about was Angel. They play basketball and video games like I do. Angel doesn't eat meat cuz he likes animals too much, just like me – except I eat meat. He doesn't take stuff because it makes his Pepsi get too bad."

"Epilepsy, Mackenzie," Elliott corrected, leaning forward to listen to his daughter for the first time in her ten-year existence. "When did you hear Willow and Gage talking?"

"The second night we were in Italy at the party with all the rainbows. You and mom were fighting again, so I went outside. They were talking on the balcony. Uncle Gage was smoking and kept pulling out a bag of white stuff."

Both Marjorie and Larry Lang's jaws were on the floor. Still, Mackenzie kept her eyes on the game in her hands. She absorbed by proximity, spilling all the family's dirty secrets in one fell swoop.

"Can I have a soda?" Mackenzie continued, oblivious to the bomb she'd just dropped on everyone. Indra was the one to finally break the tense silence by snorting once and shaking his head.

"I will get it for you, Mackenzie. Come. Pick one with me," he said, extending his hand to her as he rose from his seat beside Bella.

"Ok!" Mackenzie said happily, elated to have someone's attention. Elliott watched the man walk away with his daughter, feeling an odd twang of *jealousy* of all things in his gut. He looked at his wife, then at the rug beneath his polished shoes.

"Quinn helped Gage kick his habit in high school," Bella finally said. "He told me because... because he remembered both of us begging Elliott to quit when he was addicted too."

"Bells!" Elliott hissed.

"Oh, stop," Bella replied. "You nearly died in my arms, Elliott! You're lucky Quinn had enough intelligence to dial three little digits or you *wouldn't* be here! I'm *glad* all you do is drink. Quinn and I didn't want to see that happen again. There wasn't anything to be done for Will. She's just fucking weird, anyway. Quinn swore up and down that Angel would never do any drugs. We hid it so you wouldn't say anything, dad. We hide *everything* so you won't say anything. No one can know how fucked up we are. It isn't good for business. Paige and Elliott don't even like each other, for fuck's sake. They stay married because you pay their mortgage and their money stops if they divorce. Divorce isn't good for business either and the business you're in is good fucking face."

By the end of *her* tirade, Bella was crying. She wiped her eyes and stood, turning into her husband with a gasp of surprise. Indra stood with Mackenzie beside him, Coke in her small hands, drinking it out of a straw like nothing else mattered in the whole world.

And then it all changed.

"Bella, we are going home," Indra said. Bella nodded, shaking with fear or embarrassment or both – it was hard to tell. But Indra wasn't finished. He looked at Larry Lang with disgust on his face. "Children are cherished in my culture, not to be paraded around for show. You should be ashamed. My children will *never* return here. Nor will my wife."

The shock on Bella's face rang as clearly as a gong through the room. Indra wrapped his arm around her shoulders and led her out of the room, while the rest of them stared in stunned silence, broken only by the sounds of Mackenzie slurping at her soda.

17

Gage took up the couch for almost two whole days, sleeping like a dead man. Quinn nearly called an ambulance when he was still asleep on the morning of day three. Instead, he nearly screamed when Gage stood outside the bathroom door, waiting to go in.

"Jesus Christ! What the hell, Gage!"

"I've gotta piss," Gage grumbled, shuffling past Quinn into the bathroom. Angel had already left for work. Quinn almost felt like calling the man so he didn't have to be alone with his brother, then realized how stupid that was and shuffled to the kitchen. His phone rang just as Gage came out. It was Bella.

"Bells," Quinn said, looking at Gage. The kid shook his head. Quinn sighed, answering the phone on speaker so Gage could hear her.

"Hey, Bells."

"Hey," she replied, sounding tired. "How are you?"

That made Quinn frown. Bella never asked him how he was. Bella never called, period. The last time she called it was to 'discuss' invitations to the wedding that never happened. Thinking about it put a sour pit in Quinn's stomach.

"Fine," he replied curtly, then felt bad about it after so added, "You?"

"Ok. How's Angel?"

Again, Quinn made a face at his phone, then looked at Gage. The youngest Lang shrugged and slid silently into one of the bar stools across from where Quinn stood.

"He's fine too. Better," Quinn said.

"Good," Bella said. "Uhm… fuck it, look, have you seen Gage or heard from him? He's been gone over a week now. I'm kinda worried. I guess he blew up at dad or something and took off. No one's seen him or heard from him since. I've… I've checked."

Quinn's jaw hit the counter. So did Gage's. They looked at each other in pure shock. Quinn muted the phone.

"What the fuck? What do I tell her?" Quinn asked. Gage shrugged again, as shocked as Quinn.

"I know it's weird of me to ask. I'm just worried, you know? I don't want the same thing that happened to Elliott to happen to him too. He's just a kid, Q. Dad was making a big deal about whatever it was he did. I don't think we were really paying attention until Mackie outed everyone. Indra's so pissed. He won't let me even *talk* to dad and mom. Paige filed for divorce the day after it all went down. It's such a mess, Q, you have no idea. *Everyone* is talking about it. It's sick. Mom is beside herself. She's left me a hundred messages begging me to talk to Indra. Please, just let me know if you hear from Gage, ok?"

"Y-yeah," Quinn replied, looking right at his brother.

"Hey, whatever happens, be glad you got out when you did," Bella added. "Bye."

She hung up before Quinn could reply. Quinn stared at his phone for a good long while before looking up at Gage.

"What the hell is going on, Gage?" Quinn finally sighed. "Why come here? Why-"

"It's safe here," Gage croaked. Again, Quinn's jaw hit the counter. He was staring at an alien replacement of his brother and his sister was a robot. It was the only sane explanation for their sudden shift in personality and priorities.

"Safe? From what?" Quinn dared.

Gage shrugged.

"Mom and dad. Their bullshit. Their fucking friends and hypocrisy. Harder for me to get drugs here. I don't have a connection here. I dunno just.. safe. You guys have fish, for fuck's sake, and a place that smells normal. That's not some stupid expensive Oriental rug. It's just some piece of shit you guys probably got at Target."

"Ikea," Angel corrected from the door. Rachel stood beside him, holding him up.

"He had a seizure at work. I brought him home," she explained. Both Lang brothers merely stared for a moment before moving. Quinn came out to help Rachel get Angel to his bed while Gage watched. If Quinn hadn't just experienced the personality swings, he never would have believed that he saw guilt etched into Gage's expression.

"It's my fault," Gage said, following them all into Angel's room. Quinn frowned back at his brother. "It's my fault he's like that. I drugged him. Willow made me do it."

"What?" Quinn hissed. Gage had the decency to look at the floor while Rachel got Angel settled in the bed.

"She threatened to tell dad about... my habit. She was helping Racine. If they got rid of Angel, dad would have made you marry that hag. I'm sorry."

Quinn took two steps toward his brother with teeth bared and fists balled when Rachel intervened.

"Don't," she said quietly. "It won't change anything, Q, and Angel needs us right now."

Quinn stopped, still glowering at his brother. He took several breaths, then turned to sit with Angel where he belonged.

#

Angel remembered looking at his rug but little else until waking with his face pressed against Rachel's side. He didn't need to see her to know. He knew her scent and the feel of her. He felt light-headed but seemed none the worse for wear.

"Awake now?" Rachel whispered, gently rubbing his back. He nodded. "How do you feel?"

"Dizzy," he grumbled into her inviting body. He nuzzled into her, inhaling the smell of her to help clear his addled mind. Angel felt the rapid-fire shocks of electricity zipping across his skull, like waiting for a sleeping limb to come back to life only it happened inside his head. He hated the feeling, hated how much he felt it of late. Thirty-two years of life, probably twenty-eight of which he remembered, and his epilepsy had never been so out of control. What was worse, he had no real explanation for his doctors other than 'I don't know' when asked why he would do something so dangerous as to do drugs. He didn't do drugs. He didn't *do* anything.

"Was I dreaming when I heard Gage apologize?" Angel asked, his voice still croaking and mumbled. Rachel stroked his hair, running her fingers through it to help alleviate some of the electric shock sensations. He shut his eyes again and let her soothe him while waiting for her response.

"You weren't dreaming," she said softly. "Quinn wanted to call a cab to send him to the airport. I told him to leave it. I'm not sure if that was right or not, but he apologized and genuinely seemed to feel bad about it, Angel. Their family is so fucked up and petty. The kid really does hate it. You've seen how much Quinn hates it. I sent him to get dinner instead of beating on his brother like he wanted to do. He should be back soon."

Angel let her explanation sink in while she carded her fingers through his long hair. Part of him immediately jumped to rage that demanded payback. The rest of him just felt pure pity for that kid and their messed up family. What must it be like to grow up never knowing what it felt like to be loved? Quinn certainly managed, but just barely, and only because he got out early and went to college. If he hadn't, if he hadn't met Angel, what would have happened to him? Probably the same as Gage or worse, considering how bad his anxiety and depression could get.

"Where's Gage?" Angel dared.

"On the couch."

Angel remained where he was until nature decided he needed to move. He showered, using up all the hot water so he could stand beneath its cascading heat until all of his muscles felt properly liquified. The time in the water let him think and process all that had happened, all that had been said and done.

"Angel?" Rachel asked, slipping into the bathroom just before he was ready to turn the water off. "You ok?"

"Yeah," he said, turning the water off. He pulled the curtain back and smiled at the vision standing before him.

Rachel held a nice clean towel open for him. His mom used to do the same when he was a child, but it was not a thing that happened now as an adult. There was a lot that changed as people got older. Quinn liked to complain that no one gave out stickers to adults unless they voted. Angel made it a point to add stickers to their campaigns so people remembered *what* to vote for. The statistics showed a greater swing in their direction after the stickers were added. It was the little things, Angel found, that brought comfort, things that were forgotten as adults but brought comfort all the same. Like an inviting, open towel.

He went to Rachel, letting her wrap him up as he leaned down into her shoulder. His hair dripped all over her, but she didn't seem to mind, rubbing his back and arms with the soft warmth of the towel. Out of the pure need to touch another loving human being, Angel tilted his head into Rachel's neck, kissing it softly. She sighed contentedly, drying him off slowly so they could be close. That's all he wanted, to be close to her.

"Come on. Come back to bed," she said quietly, still holding him. He nodded into her neck, kissing it still.

She shut the door to his room, leading him to the bed with the towel around his shoulders like a cape. If Gage saw anything while he shuffled out of the bathroom, Angel didn't care. He was tired of giving a shit about what others thought; he was just *tired*.

"Come here, baby," Rachel said, as she crawled beneath the covers, as naked as he was. Her clothes were in a small pile on the floor. He was still so out of it he didn't even realize she'd undressed. Angel sighed and crawled into the bed beside her. He laid his head on her chest, listening to her heartbeat while she stroked his hair, humming a soft lullaby to him. Angel shut his eyes, listening to her semi-tuneless humming, letting it lull him into a state of meditation that emptied his mind of everything, allowing him to recenter himself.

"I love you," Angel said, with his eyes still closed. Rachel's hand stopped for a minute, then resumed its motions.

"I love you too, Angel. So much," she said in a soft whisper. Angel looked up at her, adjusting so that he was face to face with her rather than against her chest.

"Does this bother you?" he asked. He needed to know.

"What? Being with you?" Angel shook his head. "I don't understand the question then."

"Does it bother you that I love Quinn too?" he asked, forcing himself to say those words to her. He hadn't yet, letting things move slowly, like testing the waters before diving in headfirst.

"Angel, you've always loved Quinn even before you realized it. I've always seen it for as long as I've known you."

"Is that a no?" he smirked. She smiled back at him.

"That's a no," she murmured against his lips, kissing him gently. He returned the kiss, drawing her closer to him. That was where he stayed, close to her heart, kissing and touching her until Quinn returned with dinner.

#

No one spoke during dinner. No one spoke after it either. Everyone remained so silent the fish were starting to get anxious. Rachel left shortly after dinner to check on Juju, promising to return in the morning. Angel felt guilty for not going with her, but neither she nor Quinn would allow him to leave alone, nor would they allow Gage to stay in the apartment without supervision. No one trusted him. Sadly, he seemed to sense that.

"I should go," Gage said finally when the tension had grown so heavy it became suffocating.

"Probably for the best," Quinn grunted. Angel was not going to maintain this cycle of hatred Quinn's family had, however.

"It's fine. It's just couch space."

"Angel he–" Quinn started, but Angel held up his hand.

"I know. I was semi–coherent for his explanation, Quinn. I know what he did. He apologized for it too. In person, even. He didn't call or write an email or text. He flew across the country to apologize in person. Let's just… move on. Please? I don't want to keep dredging this up anymore."

"But–" Quinn argued.

"No, Quinn," Angel repeated. "Let it go."

Gage simply gaped at the two of them, earning a glower from Quinn that dropped his gaze to the floor. Angel let out a little sigh, finding that inner peace again that helped keep him calm.

"You're enrolled in school, aren't you?" Angel asked, drawing Gage's gaze back up. He nodded. "Where?"

"Stanford," he said. "Linguistics."

It was not a subject Angel expected to hear considering the demands of the Lang family values. Business or medicine, even law, but not linguistics.

"Why does it matter?" Quinn dared. He was full of rage. Angel understood why. It was easy to let that rage take over. Angel wanted to let *his* rage take over too, but all that would do would be to trigger another seizure. He needed less of those, not more. So, Angel sought the path of peace instead.

"Because he'll need to transfer his credits to Georgetown if he's going to stay," Angel explained.

"Stay?" both of the Lang brothers said, though Quinn's version was decidedly sharper in pitch than Gage's. Angel sighed.

"Yes, Quinn, stay. Or do you intend on sending him *back* to the pieces of shit that keep doing this to him and you and *me*? Huh? He didn't ask for this. Neither did you. But as far as I can tell, he's the only one with the balls to do something about it. You didn't. As a matter of fact, if I recall, you *believed* them, didn't you? Because that was easier than defending me, wasn't it?"

Quinn shut his mouth with a click.

"So, Gage gets the couch until we can find a bigger place," Angel finished, looking at Gage. "But I *will* kick your ass through the first window I see if you get high again, *entiendes*?"

"Yeah, I understand," Gage nodded. Quinn gaped again.

"Why do you understand him?!"

"Linguistics," Angel and Gage said together. Quinn merely huffed off to his room, slamming it shut.

#

Quinn spent two whole days grumping around the apartment like an angry troll. Halfway through the third day, the phone rang again, his sister's name prominently displayed on the screen. Quinn sighed, answering on speaker. No one was home anyway. Angel took the rest of the week off work for his health and sanity. He decided after lunch to take Gage out for clean clothes so the kid would stop borrowing theirs.

"Hey, Bells," Quinn said as he answered on

speaker like he always did while working.

"The cops just arrested Willow, Q," Bella said in an almost accusatory manner.

"What? Why? What'd she do now?" Quinn asked. It was not the first time their sister had a run-in with the authorities. She was the wild child, the one dancing on bars and giving the paparazi a good show.

"Intent on committing murder, Quinn! And financial shit cuz she gave Racine money – to commit murder! She's being blamed for Angel's bullshit!" Bella barked.

"What? Whoa, ok, hold on, why are you yelling at *me* because she's getting in trouble for what happened to him? I didn't turn her in!"

"Turn her in? Quinn, what the fuck is going on!" Bella snarled. Quinn hung up. Angel was right. They couldn't send Gage back to that shit show.

The devil appeared shortly thereafter, laughing. It was a sound Quinn did not recall hearing much of before now. He forced himself to take a steadying breath and pushed away from his workstation. He wasn't actually working. Each screen had a different house prominently displayed on it, each of them near or in DC proper. Quinn left them up, going out to the living room to meet his boyfriend and his brother.

Each of them had at least four bags in

each hand, filling the floor space with thrift-store finds. Angel never bought anything at the mall like a normal person. He said it was wasteful. Just watching him made Quinn relax and smirk.

"Your boy knows how to get all the best deals, bro. This shit is *lit*," Gage said. Quinn merely blinked. Much like Spanish, he didn't speak jive either. Angel noticed and tried not to smirk, but Quinn caught it anyway.

"Well, now you can keep your lit gear and stop taking ours," Angel said, moving through the finds to the kitchen for a glass of water. He gave Quinn's shoulder a squeeze as he went by. The sudden feeling of guilt hit Quinn like a hammer. He'd been an ass the last two days, feeling oddly betrayed by the person that *should* be angry but wasn't.

"What's wrong?" Angel asked, coming to stand beside him. Quinn shrugged, caught Angel's eye and shuffled silently back to his room. Angel followed. "Quinn?"

"How do you do it?" Quinn asked, staring at the houses on the screens.

"Do what?"

"Forgive so easily?" Quinn asked. "I want so badly to hate him for what he did to you. Hate myself for not believing you. Hate my family for being assholes. But you... you're just..."

"It isn't worth the energy to hate them, Q," Angel explained softly. "You know, what happened sucks. I'm still paying for it. But I got to see Italy. I got to meet the sweetest little girl ever, that absolutely loves animals. I got a better understanding of why you are the way you are."

Quinn snorted, looking up at Angel when the man moved closer.

"I got you," he said. Quinn felt his face heat up. "It's a matter of finding the good in all the bad. Who knows, maybe your brother will stay clean this time and find someone *he* loves. You'll start a whole new trend."

Quinn snorted, looking down at their feet. His socks were simple white with the gray toe. Hanes. Angel's socks didn't match. One was burgundy with pickles on it, the other navy and green stripes. They were so different yet so perfect for each other it physically hurt Quinn to think about.

"Bella called the other day asking if I knew where Gage was. I didn't tell her. He was sitting with me when she called. She called again today while you were out with him. Willow's been arrested for attempted murder or something."

"Wow. Of who?"

"You," Quinn said, looking up at Angel again. The shock on his face might have been comical in any other situation.

"Me? She didn't do–"

"She's the one that told Gage to drug you and must have done something else too. Guess you missed that part," Quinn said.

"Oh..."

Quinn raked a hand through his hair, turning toward the screens. Angel looked too, leaning forward to get a better look at the five houses displayed on the screens.

"Quinn, all these houses cost over two million dollars."

"Yeah..." Quinn said, trying to understand what the problem was.

"Quinn! We are not buying a two–million dollar home!"

"Why not? They're nice, and they're nearby still. That one isn't even a million, it's only nine–twenty–five," Quinn argued. Angel's eyes bugged out of his head. "Well, what else am I supposed to do with my money if I'm not allowed to spend it?"

"Are you kidding?" Angel said.

"Angel, I buy *ramen*. You pay half the rent and half our bills. I think the last time I bought myself clothes before going to Italy was when we *graduated*. Where do you think my allowance has all gone to?"

"I... hadn't really thought about it because

until a few months ago, I didn't know you were getting one," he retorted.

"Exactly. So if we're doing this, then let me do this. Let me buy you something nice; something big enough to host your insanely large family for a change."

Angel snorted out a laugh that made Quinn smile. He loved that laugh, loved every part of Angel Rivera.

"I'm not cleaning something big enough to host my family," Angel smiled. Quinn reached out and took his hand, pulling him in for a sweet, and much needed, kiss. "What was that for?"

"For being you, and helping me be me," Quinn answered, kissing Angel more soundly.

"Your brother's out in the living room," Angel cautioned. Quinn nodded.

"He's a big kid. He can babysit himself for a bit," Quinn said, kissing Angel again.

18

"**F**UCK!" Quinn cried. Angel laughed, shushing him even as he moved in and out of Quinn's slightly sore ass. They'd been fucking for over an hour, 'christening' their new home. Boxes were stacked against a wall in every room. Furniture had been delivered the day before and all the new stuff wasn't due until the day after. They'd moved from a two-bedroom apartment to a six-bedroom townhome on Massachusetts Avenue. Gage got his own space in the basement and Rachel took the second master suite.

"God, Angel..." Quinn panted, moaning as the man rocked in and out of him in time to the strokes he was giving Quinn's cock. "Angel..."

"We're making a mess on purpose, remember? Just cum for me, Quinn."

"GOD!" Quinn shouted mere seconds after

being told what to do. Angel continued pumping him in his hand, moving in and out until finally reaching his own climax, biting down hard on Quinn's shoulder, which made Quinn orgasm a second time. Quinn twisted around to kiss Angel, sucking in a sharp breath when the bedroom door opened.

"You know, it's not fair of you guys to make so much noise without inviting me," Rachel said. She stood silhouetted in the doorway. Quinn was so mortified he didn't know whether to hide or crawl away to the bathroom.

"Since when did you need an invitation?" Angel replied, making Quinn's face heat up like a teakettle.

"Since I can see how red Q is getting even in the dark," Rachel teased. Quinn hid his face in the pillow as Angel pulled out and rolled off the bed to go to Rachel.

"Well, it was bound to happen at some point. Might as well be while we christen the new house, right?" Angel said, bringing Rachel back to the bed. Quinn whipped his head around to look at his boyfriend and his boyfriend's girlfriend. The logistics were a little dizzying.

"Uhm..." Quinn started, watching Angel drop the robe Rachel wore off her shoulders. "What are you doing?"

"Bringing Rachel into the fun, Q. You don't have to do anything, I promise," Angel said.

"I don't either. I was just teasing you two. You're a little loud," Rachel said. "I thought it was just an Italy thing. Mind if I just watch? Kinda curious."

"Seriously?" Angel chortled.

"What? I've never seen two guys do it before," she said. Angel kept laughing. She smacked his bare chest. Quinn wanted to die.

"That is all on Quinn," Angel laughed. "Q?"

"God, why are you doing this to me?" Quinn said into the pillow. He flinched when Angel kissed his shoulder.

"Relax," Angel said kindly. "We don't have to do anything you don't want to."

"How 'bout a bath then?" Rachel suggested. "God knows yours is the size of a damn pool."

It was. Not that Rachel didn't also have a bathtub, but the one in their suite was much larger than hers. Hers was cute, dainty, and entirely Victorian; theirs was a massive rectangular piece of modern art.

"I can do a bath," Quinn finally agreed. He ran the water, filling it with bubbles for Rachel's benefit while she and Angel had a little bit of private time. Seeing Rachel naked only confirmed – again – that Quinn had no desire to be with a woman. She was pretty enough, but there was nothing at all enticing about her form like there was in Angel's.

The water helped relax them, let them enjoy each other's company without expectation for anything more. Despite all of that, Quinn still felt a little possessive, pulling Angel into his arms to rub his back and shoulders, relishing in how the man relaxed against him. He traced every line of Angel's beautiful tattoos, massaging them gently.

"That feels good," Angel rumbled. Quinn continued, kissing Angel's neck, running soapy hands along his arms. He only paused long enough to glance up at Rachel when she moved forward, wrapping her legs around Angel's.

"What if we worked together to make him feel good?" Rachel said. Quinn thought on it a moment, and finally nodded. Rachel kissed Angel while Quinn rubbed his back, reaching around to caress his chest, his hand grazing Rachel's breasts. She didn't pull away, moving closer still. Quinn caught on quicker than most gave him credit for. Rachel was slick.

"Lift up," Quinn said against Angel's ear while Rachel kissed him. Angel complied, settling on Quinn's lap. Quinn's cock slipped between Angel's cheeks, letting him grind gently until he was hard and slick with the soapy bubbles. Only then did he line himself up with Angel's waiting hole, pressing himself in until the head of his cock broke through.

Angel moaned into Rachel's mouth, groaning as Quinn continued to press in until he was seated to the hilt. Rachel stroked Angel off until he was hard again, climbing on top of them both when she was satisfied with Angel's erection.

"Oh shit..." Angel groaned. "Guys..."

"Shhh," Rachel said, gently. "Enjoy it, baby. You deserve it."

Part of Quinn wanted to be embarrassed. The other part was thrilled to be doing something different-ish. The majority, however, simply felt elated to be bringing Angel pleasure.

All three of them rocked together, Rachel milking Angel from the front while Quinn fucked him from behind. Hearing Angel moan made Quinn want to do more, rock harder, and faster, setting a pace that had the bathwater sloshing around them, adding to the sensation.

"Guys..." Angel groaned again, his muscles tensing beneath Quinn's hands. "Oh, fuck, guys!"

"Let it go, Angel. I want to take it all!" Rachel said, rocking harder, grinding on him so that Angel ground into Quinn.

"Jesus!" Quinn hissed, exploding inside of Angel as a result. He felt a wave of gooseflesh race across Angel's skin as his only warning before Angel's muscles contracted over Quinn's cock. "FUCK!"

"Yes, baby!" Rachel cried, continuing her grind until she was orgasming as well. "Oh, God! Oh, God!"

Any noise Angel might have made was lost inside of Quinn's mouth. He tugged Angel back enough to claim the other man's mouth. They remained attached to each other, moving even after their climax until each of them orgasmed again, and again. Then, they moved their party back to the bed. It lasted well into the late hours of the morning, with Rachel and Quinn focusing all of their attention on Angel.

After the house was successfully christened, the three settled into bed for well-earned sleep. Except, Quinn couldn't sleep. He watched Angel sleep, nuzzled in between himself and Rachel. That was when he noticed that Rachel wasn't sleeping either. She smiled at him, glancing down at Angel almost wistfully.

"Is this really happening?" Quinn asked, in awe of their situation. Rachel's smile narrowed her eyes even more, but she nodded.

"Yeah, Q, it is. Do you know why?" she asked. Quinn frowned and shook his head. "Because we may both need him, but he *wants* us. I knew as soon as I met this nerd that I was doomed. I bet you did too. But he makes the active choice to love both of us, flaws and all."

"Rachel, you're perfect. What is there to possibly not love about you? All he does is gush about you," Quinn snorted.

"Funny, he does the same for you," she countered. "I can't give him what he wants most." Quinn frowned again. "Kids, Quinn. I can't give him kids."

"What?"

"He didn't tell you, did he?" she asked. He shook his head. "I can't have them. Really rare birth defect. There's nothing there to make a baby with. He loves me anyway. I couldn't ask for anything more than that."

Quinn remained silent after that, letting Rachel's words process while the sun came up through the window at his back.

#

Larry Lang looked into his brandy glass, swirling the dark liquid without actually seeing it. Maximillian Fier sat across from him, watching every reaction with a critical eye. The country clubs were all still abuzz with the incident in Italy over Quinn's not-wedding and the resulting scandal that rocked the community. Larry lost out on two deals because of that debacle. If not for Indra, he would have lost out on another one, but the oil prince of Dubai was quick with words and explanations, even if he'd kept his word about keeping Bella and the kids away. Business was business. Marjorie had already spent a fortune with the therapists, or at the shops with all the people that were 'so embarrassed' to be involved in something so dramatic while also consoling herself. It was a complete mess.

"Honestly, Larry, there isn't really much to think about. This is your reputation on the line. I'm doing you a favor," Maximillian said. The smirk that curled the man's lips was meant to be hidden. Larry pretended not to notice.

"Yeah, I know," Larry finally sighed. He drained the brandy after that.

"Then why the hesitation?" Maximillian pressed. Larry shrugged, looking through the brandy glass again. Quinn's last words to him still struck a surprising chord he never thought he'd feel in his long, privileged life: fear. He didn't understand it. He had nothing to fear. Even without Maximillian's 'generous' offer, the Langs would pull through with heads held high, as they always had. Yes, their reputations may come out a little tarnished, but that was worth having his family *intact* – wasn't it?

The answer should have been an easy one,

yet was the furthest thing from easy Larry could think of. He'd paid Willow's bail and sent a pack of lawyers at the Los Angeles D.A. like hounds on the hunt for defamation of character. There was no evidence to charge his daughter with what they'd claimed she'd done. Willow was eccentric, but she wasn't a murderer nor conspirator. She certainly didn't have the wherewithal to commit any financial crimes. There was a reason the poor girl was a model.

The honest truth was that things were in total shambles. He put on a good face, held his head as high as he could, but the worry was starting to drag him down from the lofty point of privilege in which he normally existed.

No one had heard from Gage in over a month. Mackenzie was living under *his* roof because of the nasty divorce Paige was bringing upon Elliott. While Indra would not allow Bella to come home, she called from time to time to check on Marjorie's state of mental health, which was worse than Larry allowed himself to believe. Then, there was Quinn.

"Larry?" Maximillian prompted. Larry wasn't aware that the man had been talking. He stood from his seat and sighed, moving to the door.

"I'll talk to Quinn, Maxie. We'll be in touch."

19

Elliott Lang watched his daughter play on the swings in their massive back yard. He had the play set installed when the girl was only two and never gave it a second thought. The divorce was already ugly. Paige demanded half of what Elliott had, and claimed the pregnancy was forced so she wanted nothing to do with Mackenzie. Elliott wasn't sure he did either, but only because he had no clue what to do with his daughter. She'd been with his parents for the past few weeks while Elliott sorted things out. He was never home, always at the hospital or else at a bar, normally. He'd literally missed the girl's entire life.

"Dr. Lang?" the lawyer said. Elliott looked at the woman and smiled. He took the pen she held out to him and signed the document in front of him. He had to update the will and a few other things because of what Paige was pulling. A whole team of lawyers was ready to fight his cursed wife in court. She wouldn't walk away with a single penny if Elliott had his way.

"We'll get these filed right away," the lawyer finished. The look she gave was a subtle invitation that had Elliott hard in his pants in an instant and the lawyer bent over his desk within minutes. He needed the release, taking the woman from behind with her skirt hiked up around her waist and tight blouse open. Her breasts pressed against his desk and her open, moaning mouth left steam against the high sheen of the wood.

It lasted minutes. Most of his trysts were like that. Fleeting moments of time that he never thought about again. The woman left shortly thereafter. Elliott hired a nanny as soon as he realized his only other option for childcare was his parents. When Sofia arrived, Elliott brought Mackenzie home. Sofia was cute too, young, from Italy where he'd met her at a bar one night that he managed to slip away. She was elated with the job and gave him some nice benefits beneath the sheets from time to time. It was a good deal all around.

"Mackenzie! Come inside please!" Elliott called once he'd cleaned himself up. Sofia had lunch ready for them and smiled when Mackenzie came in.

Elliott let his daughter eat lunch, then had Sofia clean it up before taking the girl out to the back deck with an ice cream to soften the blow of what he needed to say.

"So, we need to have a chat, Mackie," he began.

"Are you leaving too?" Mackenzie asked with about as much emotion as one might have if they were asking for apples. Elliott stared at her for a while, jaw hanging open, before coming to his senses.

"You're too smart for your own good, kiddo. I am but I'm leaving because I need to – *want* to get better. For you. For me. Sorta... give us a shot at something a little more normal. Sofia will be here with you until I get back, ok?"

Mackenzie nodded, licking the ice cream off the spoon. She was so innocent still.

"Mackie, if you could go anywhere right now, where would you go?"

"Disneyland!" she smiled with mischief in her big brown eyes. Elliott laughed and nodded.

"That's a pretty fun place. Who would you go with?"

Mackenzie thought about it for a minute, the spoon in her mouth while her mind worked through the very short list of people she'd been exposed to. Paige was very particular about being seen with Mackenzie, as if doing so might tarnish some weird reputation his ex insisted on maintaining.

"Uncle Quinn and Angel. They're really fun to be around," Mackenzie finally answered. It made Elliott smile, made the knot in his stomach ease up a little.

One task down, Elliott collected his luggage and said goodbye to his daughter. He needed to do this, to finally and truly get sober and find a direction that was *separate* from what his parents demanded. In fact, he went to their house to tell them so after leaving Mackenzie in Sofia's capable hands. As expected, they did not take the news well.

"Elliott, I don't understand. *Why* do you feel the need to go into rehab! You're *fine*!" Marjorie Lang practically screeched. "What will the community *say*!"

"Mom, I don't care what they say. I haven't for a while. I'm doing this for *me*. I wake up drunk, go through the day drunker, and repeat the entire process all over again the following day. That's a serious problem. I'm a neurosurgeon, for fuck's sake, but I *need* liquor to keep a steady hand while operating. I can't do this anymore."

"But Paige–"

"Left me," Elliott cut off.

"And Mackenzie?" Larry Lang butt in. Elliott looked at his father with narrowed eyes.

"She's fine. She's in good hands. You don't need to worry about her."

"Elliott, she's–"

"Fine, dad," Elliott cut in again. "I already put things in order for you. If anything happens to me, you won't need to worry at all about Mackenzie. In fact, I would rather you forget about her entirely, just like you forgot about the rest of us."

"Elliot!" Marjorie wailed.

"Elliott, that's not fair. We've–"

"Done everything for me. I know. You won't let me forget it. I don't need you to pay my mortgage. I don't need you to watch my daughter. I don't need *you* for anything anymore. I'm going to be in rehab for however long it takes me to get clean. I'm telling you as a courtesy, not as a request for permission. I'm forty fucking years old. I think I'm allowed to make my own decisions. Maybe when things are better, we can talk about rebuilding a relationship but, right now, I'd rather not have anything to do with either of you. Stay away from my daughter."

Elliott didn't say anything more, leaving to the sound of his mother's wails and desperate pleas to be mindful of what people might think of *her*.

It would be the last time anyone saw Elliott Lang alive.

#

The phone rang through the quiet room at the unholy hours of the morning. The only reason Angel knew this was because he and Quinn had only *just* gone to sleep after a few rounds of hot and heavy sex. The room still smelled of it, Quinn's ringtone echoing against the marble walls. Angel heard it first, groaning at his lover to answer the phone. In reality, it mostly came out as a muttered slur of syllables that had no real definition. When the phone stopped, Angel merely sighed and rolled deeper into his pillows.

Then, it began ringing again.

"Quinn," Angel slurred.

"Mm?"

"Phone?"

"Mm."

Angel absently reached behind him to smack Quinn in a vain attempt to wake the Asian man from sleep. When his poor attempts failed, Angel sat up with a frown on his face, eyes still closed and grabbed the phone from the same spot it always sat – right beside Quinn's head.

"'Lo?" he said without looking at the caller.

"No s'his boyfriend. – – Angel. – – Why? Who is this?"

The more he spoke, the more his head cleared until he was actively smacking Quinn on the arm to wake him. The Seattle police were calling.

"What?" Quinn growled, rolling over to glower at Angel.

"Get up. The Seattle police are on the phone," Angel said, putting the call on speaker between them. "No, I'm still here. We both are. What, exactly, is this regarding?"

"Elliot Lang. He's Quinn Lang's elder brother, I believe. The man had a living will to inform Mr. Lang in the event of an emergency."

"He what?" Quinn blurted. Angel smacked Quinn's bare chest again. Quinn frowned at him.

"Detective, has something happened?"

"I'm afraid so, and I hate making calls like this, especially since it seems I woke you. Elliott Lang was in a car accident this evening. Social services is waiting at his home with his daughter. Mr. Lang is listed as her next of kin."

Quinn gaped.

They were on the next flight out to Seattle with little more than shouted explanations given to Rachel and Gage. By the time they reached Elliott Lang's home, the sun was starting to come up over the horizon on the west coast. The place was massive, covered in lush green ivy. Cop cars sat in the U-shaped driveway, with officers barricading the front door. Both Angel and Quinn had to show ID before being allowed into the old brick home. Floor-to-ceiling windows let in endless amounts of natural sunlight that washed Mackenzie out in an angelic halo. Bella sat with her, eyes rimmed red from crying.

"Jesus, Bells," Quinn said as he went to his sister. Angel went to Mackenzie.

"Quinn, I don't know what's happening! Everything is falling apart! Elliott... he was going to rehab, Q! He was going to get clean!" Bella sobbed.

Mackenzie looked up at Angel with sorrow in her big eyes but detached understanding as well. She was a smart kid. He doubted there was much that got by her. Angel said nothing, squatting in front of her. She threw her arms around his neck and sobbed like Bella did on Quinn. She understood, and it broke Angel's heart.

"What's with the barricade?" Quinn asked, still holding his sister.

"Mom and dad keep coming by. Elliott made it *real* clear that he didn't want them in the house or near Mackenzie. Sofia called me because she didn't know who else to call. He was really trying, Q. I just… why is this happening?"

"I dunno, Bells," Quinn sighed, looking over at Angel. Angel had no answers either, feeling oddly responsible for the run of bad luck the Langs were suffering through.

Bella was not wrong, however, and neither was the detective that rocked them from sleep with terrible news. Elliott's living will – recently redone – cut everyone out of the will *except* Mackenzie. As the divorce never finalized, it left Paige a penniless widow who was also barred from seeing her daughter; not that the woman tried. As if sensing something might go wrong, Elliott appointed Quinn as Mackenzie's guardian.

They stayed a week for the funeral, helped Bella and Sofia get Mackenzie's things in order, then finally flew home to DC without once seeing Quinn's parents. The hateful duo managed to respect their late son's wishes and remained absent.

Once home, Mackenzie stood in the foyer of their new house, holding Angel and Sofia's hands. Rachel and Gage met them, both looking hopeful for Mackenzie's sake.

"Wanna pick your room, kiddo?" Gage finally said after clearing his throat. Mackenzie looked at him but held tighter to Angel's hand.

"Why don't I go too? I still get lost in this

place. Sofia can come pick a room too," Angel offered. Mackenzie nodded, letting them lead her away. As they left, Angel heard Quinn finally break down, sobbing on Rachel's shoulder for the loss of his brother.

239

20

"Goddammit!" Quinn growled. His voice echoed down the hall from the man's office. The slam of the keyboard followed with the click–clack of smaller things bouncing across the wood floors.

Angel's motions at the kitchen counter slowed. He looked across the breakfast bar to where Rachel and Gage sat, then toward the direction of the frustrated snarl. Mackenzie glanced up from the game she played with Sofia long enough to throw a concerned look of her own at the odd grouping of people that now played the role of parents. The girl had been with them for almost two weeks, quietly settling into their lives.

"I got him last time," Rachel said. Angel sighed, set down the carrot and knife, and wiped his hands. He made the slow trek toward Quinn's office, careful not to squash Rachel's stupid dog. The yappy little thing got underfoot anytime someone moved. The three lovers were supposed to be heading out to a cookout with Gage and Mackenzie to introduce them to their friends and, hopefully, help Gage make some new ones. Instead, they waited for Quinn to finish working – something that was, apparently, not going well.

Things had been relatively stressful since the tragedy that took Elliott's life. It *was* an accident. While his alcohol levels had been elevated, it was the semi-truck that slammed into him at sixty miles an hour that took the man's life, through no fault of his own. Angel took leave from work to be with Mackenzie and Rachel switched up her schedule to two days in office and three at home to help with the little girl as much as she could. Granted, they had Sofia, but none of them wanted Mackenzie growing up with the nanny as her primary caregiver. The stress, however, was starting to send Quinn over the edge.

"Q?" Angel hazarded. Four little keys lay strewn across the floor.

"What?" Quinn snapped as he snatched them up into his palm.

"How 'bout you take a break and we go eat, relax, have a drink, and you come back at this fresh tomorrow?"

"Look, if you guys want to go, then go. I need to get this done, Angel. Some of us actually work for a living," Quinn snarled. The comment immediately made Angel's ire rise. Of all the people to bark such a statement at him, Quinn was the last one Angel expected to hear it from. Angel was on leave for *Quinn's* niece, not being some lazy bum in the house.

"What is wrong with you? You've been acting like a dick for the past week," Angel finally blurted. Quinn remained soft-spoken and complacent on most things. The only thing he'd grown a backbone for was his position in bed – he liked to top and liked it more when Rachel helped turn Angel into a puddle of sweat and cum.

"I'm busy," Quinn replied just as his phone buzzed along the desk. Angel watched his partner grab the tiny machine and lob it against the wall so hard it shattered.

"What the hell, Quinn?!"

"Guys?" Rachel said from the kitchen. "You ok?"

"Fine!" they both said with decidedly different tones in their voices. Quinn's continued to be filled with rage and frustration while Angel's now carried a hint of concern. Angel even walked to the door, met Rachel's eye, and then quietly shut the door to Quinn's office.

"Want to tell me what this is about now?" Angel pressed.

"Not really," Quinn grumbled, sitting back down with a heavy flop to shove the keys back onto the keyboard. Angel frowned. He was not willing to give up that easily. So, rather than fight with a machine, Angel went to the wall and unplugged it. "Angel, what the fuck!"

"I'll plug it back in after you tell me what's wrong. I'll even leave you alone and go to the cookout *without* you and have fun *without* you since you insist on being a jack-ass. So, talk, or you don't get your cord back. I'll take it with me."

"Really?" Quinn scoffed. Angel remained stoic. Quinn gaped. "Angel, I need that to–"

"Uhm... guys?" Rachel said, her face pressed to the door by how her voice sounded muffled against the wood. They both looked at each other, then the door, but it was Angel that opened it. Rachel looked up at him with concern in her big eyes. "Mr. Lang is here."

"What?" Angel said, opening the door just enough to peek out at his kitchen nook where Mr. Lang stood. Gage and Sofia had Mackenzie tucked between them. "You have got to be fucking kidding me."

"What?" Quinn asked, coming up behind Angel. Suddenly, all of Quinn's mood swings clicked into place, including the destruction of his brand-new phone. Angel simply shut the door again and turned to face Quinn, leaning against the door, blocking the handle. "What?"

Angel hesitated, squeezing the handle tight in his fist before releasing the tension. "Your dad's here."

Quinn's jaw tightened so much Angel heard it crack.

"I told you we should've blocked our address from being listed," Quinn hissed.

"Something tells me that wouldn't have done much, Q," Angel sighed. "Is that what the phone was about? And your attitude recently? Is he here for Gage? He can't possibly be here for Mackenzie."

Quinn remained silent, but began pacing. That was *exactly* what all that was about. Angel had half a mind to call the police and issue a harassment order on Larry Lang. Logic won, however, as it usually did. Usually.

"Fine. We go out there together," Angel said. "He wants to talk, he can talk to both of us instead of cornering you *or* Gage alone so he can browbeat you into God only knows what. And he is absolutely *not* going anywhere with that poor child. I'll deck him before I let that happen. Deal?"

"I know what he's here to tell me, Angel,"

Quinn rasped out. "He's cut a deal with Maxie Fier. Bella's been calling nonstop for the past week because that's all Racine has been talking about – the 'talk' my dad and hers had about us. I just haven't wanted to deal with it with everything that's happening now."

Angel's jaw hit the floor, and his stomach tightened. "He knows we're together, though, right?"

Quinn didn't look up from the floor.

"Quinn?"

Silence.

Angel didn't know whether to be furious or crushed. Neither truly surfaced, allowing him to nod in numb shock as he stepped away from the door. When Quinn left the room, Angel remained, the cord to the computer still held in his hand. He wasn't sure how long he stood there before Rachel and Mackenzie joined him, quietly taking the stupid cord from him.

"Wanna just order pizza and watch anime tonight?" Rachel asked. "My treat."

He looked at her, blinking for the first time since Quinn left the room. The light from the window was in a different position, but Angel could still hear voices echoing through his house – the house *Quinn* bought for him. Mackenzie looked up at him with a smile on her face.

"Felt weird just sitting out there while they talked. Gage is hiding in the basement with Sofia. Figured you wouldn't mind the company," Rachel shrugged. She held her stupid dog like a football while her other hand held Angel's lightly. "You ok?"

"He never told them," Angel croaked. "About us. He didn't tell them."

"Oh..."

"Why do I keep doing this, Rae?" Angel finally asked. "Why... why do I let *them* keep doing this?"

"Because you love him and you've been doing it since you were eighteen without even knowing it," Rachel smiled. Angel frowned curiously at her. She giggled. "Leti told me. You know she likes romance movies too? And has the *best* makeup tips."

"It scares me how much time you spend with her now," Angel sighed, rubbing his brow. Rachel giggled again. Angel smirked, pulling Rachel into his arms despite the growl from her attack chihuahua. He needed the comfort, the reminder that he wasn't alone and never would be no matter what Quinn or his absurd family did or did not do. He felt Mackenzie join the hug and smiled, reaching one of his arms around to squeeze her tight too.

"Go on," Rachel said into his chest. "Go save

him before you give yourself a migraine from guilt."

"I hate that you support me like you do," he muttered into her hair, inhaling the sweet, flowery scent of it. "You're supposed to be telling me to ditch his ass and run off with you."

"I do tell you to run off with me. While dragging him along," she added. Angel smirked. Mackenzie giggled and looked up at them both. Most would scream about the unconventional home they'd brought the child into. Mackenzie saw only a group of people that doted on her every second of the day. Angel loved Rachel and Quinn both, needed them both, perhaps not in identical ways, but in ways that complemented each other, and Mackenzie was rapidly worming her way into his heart as an angel sent from heaven above to give him the children he could not physically have. "Go on, go get him."

Angel sighed but finally relented. He walked out to find Quinn pacing, biting at his fingers while his father spoke to someone on the phone by the window in the den. When Quinn noticed Angel, he stopped pacing. The look on his face was decidedly dejected.

"Did you tell him?" Angel asked quietly, without moving closer. Quinn's eyes flicked to Rachel and Mackenzie, who Angel knew hovered behind him. Quinn shook his head. Angel snorted and tried to keep his temper in check.

"It wouldn't have made a difference, Angel," Quinn said. He glanced over at his father, then back at Angel. "He asked what I wanted."

Angel didn't understand the statement. "Isn't that good?"

Quinn shook his head again. "It means he's scheming. I told him to leave me alone. Write me out of the will or whatever, just leave us alone and pretend we never existed. He said that wasn't an option and asked again."

"Quinn, I don't get what–"

"I told him he'd bury me if he made me marry Racine, Angel," Quinn hissed, shaking enough that Angel noticed it. "I meant it when I said it, and I still do."

Angel wasn't sure he heard correctly. Quinn looked at the floor.

"You don't *have* to do what he says, Quinn. Jesus, how many times do I have to tell you that!" Angel hissed.

"How many times do *we* have to tell you that?" Rachel added, moving in to stand beside Angel, holding Mackenzie's hand. They both looked at Rachel. She met their gaze and squared her shoulders, muttering something about stupid men, then pushed her way through them, leaving Mackenzie with Angel. The girl immediately took his hand and watched. "Mr. Lang."

"Rachel!" Quinn hissed. She ignored him.

"Mr. Lang," Rachel repeated until the man looked at her. "Can I ask what, exactly, the whole purpose of you coming out here was? Things didn't exactly end well last time you were near your son *or* his partner."

"It's a family matter," Mr. Lang answered.

"With all due respect, this *is* my family, Mr. Lang. So if it concerns them, then it concerns me too. Quinn and Angel have made their choices abundantly clear from the beginning."

"Their choices? They *lied*, Ms. Givens, and made a mockery of everything we were doing for them."

"Does that look like a lie to you?" Rachel said, gesturing to Quinn and Angel; to Mackenzie. "Does that *lie* look like something your eldest would entrust his only child to?"

Quinn practically hid behind Angel, beating his head between Angel's shoulder blades while squeezing Angel's other hand so hard it was starting to go numb.

"Do I need to remind you of what *everyone* in that castle heard that night?" Rachel continued.

"Oh my God, Rachel, please stop," Quinn groaned.

"Because that didn't sound like a lie to

me," she continued. "Should I point out that your youngest son *left* of his own volition because of how fabulously fucked up your *family* is?"

"Rachel..." Quinn whined. Angel kept his mouth shut, silently supporting every word Rachel spoke. He caught a glimpse of Gage and Sofia hovering out in the hall, but didn't let on.

"Young lady—"

"Please let me just stop you right there," Rachel cut in. "The only one that gets to call me that is my father, which you, thank God, are not. I don't know why you decided to show up today, but I'm done with this. I refuse to have your negativity fill my house. I need you to leave."

Angel merely smirked, meeting Mr. Lang's gaze when the man looked at him. Quinn may not be able to say what he wanted, but Rachel did not have that problem. Neither did Angel.

"Enjoy the rest of your day, Mr. Lang," he added with enough finality that the elder man gaped until finally leaving with an echoing slam of the front door.

"That was so lit..." Gage said from his corner when the echo finally diminished. Mackenzie giggled.

#

"Did you talk to him?" Marjorie Lang asked as her husband walked through the door to their suite in the Nation's capital. He ignored her, removing his jacket as he walked to the bar near the balcony. She watched him pour himself a drink from the crystal decanter full of fine brandy. Larry downed it in one gulp, then refilled the tumbler, this time adding two single cubes of ice. "Larry?"

"It's a nice house," the man gruffed out. Marjorie watched him move out to the balcony, unbuttoning his shirt. She frowned at his back, then stomped out behind him.

"Lawrence Lang, you did not come all the way out here to look at a house. You wouldn't know a nice house if it bit you on your behind. Now what did he say?"

"He told me to leave, Marjorie. No, actually Angel's... girlfriend – the plump girl that was there in Italy with them. *She* told me to leave. They're all living together with Mackenzie *and* Gage! He's been with them for the last few months."

"I'm sorry," Marjorie said, pressing her fingers to her temple. "Did you say Angel's girlfriend? I thought he was gay."

The look her husband threw back at her made Marjorie blink defiantly, back straightening. She did not like being made the fool. Neither did her husband. Yet, as far as she could tell, that was exactly what was happening with Quinn and his so-called beau.

"I didn't stay to get the details, Marjie, I just... I'm so tired of this, dammit. Our whole family is falling apart. First Quinn, then Willow, Gage, now Elliott? For what? A gentleman's deal? Nothing was ever written down. Look at how Elliott and Paige were – they hated each other. Always did, apparently; he wrote her out of the will! Did we really do that to them?"

"Have you lost your mind? Our children would be in poverty right now if not for us. We did them all a favor," Marjorie argued. Larry snorted back at her.

"Did we? Did we, really? I don't know, Marjorie. I'm not so sure anymore."

Marjorie took in a calming breath and forced herself to remain rational. Words were exchanged; upsetting words, by the sound of it. Larry Lang was not a defeatist, yet he stood before her with slumped shoulders and a tumbler full of brandy, holding it like a shield.

"This ends today," Marjorie said. She spun on her heel, shoes echoing through the marble flooring of the hotel suite as she grabbed up her coat and stormed out to settle this once and for all.

21

Marjorie Lang stood outside of the townhouse her son purchased, with pursed lips and an arched brow. It was rather bland on the outside. The off-white facade was offset by black window frames and doors. The landscaping out front seemed overgrown with one sad little bench beneath a tree that needed to go. She snorted and walked up the steps, pumps echoing against the porch.

Marjorie raised her hand, rapping on the door in quick succession while looking around at the chintz left out on the porch. Umbrella bucket, a shoe rack, and then she heard the yipping bark of a dog in the house. Her jaw clenched.

"… no, Juju," the demon with the angel wings said as he opened the door. "Mrs. Lang?"

"Hello, Angel," she said, trying to step inside.

He did not allow her entrance. She huffed. "Is Quinn home?"

"He's working," Angel said with a stern look on his face. "Is there something I can do for you?"

"Yes, you can let me speak with my son," Marjorie retorted in clipped tones. The tiny beast at his ankle barked again. He did not stop the creature this time.

"I don't really think that's a good idea," Angel said.

"I don't really care what *you* think, Angel. You've caused enough trouble in my family. I'm here to put a stop to it," Marjorie replied. Angel had the audacity to frown at her.

"*I've* caused enough trouble? Your son has so much anxiety and repressed depression, I'm surprised he's still a functional human being. Your *son*, Mrs. Lang. The person you should be doing everything in your power to love and protect, and *I'm* the one causing trouble? You're bat shit. You *and* your husband. And it stops now. You're not welcome here, Mrs. Lang. If you really want to talk to Quinn, change your attitude first. Have a nice afternoon."

The cretin shut the door in Marjorie's face, leaving her gaping like a fish on the stoop of an overpriced townhouse.

#

"Who was at the door?" Quinn asked as Angel came back into the living room. Mackenzie and Rachel sat beside Quinn, both now looking at Angel with concern. They'd opted to take a rain check on the cookout after Mr. Lang's visit. Angel did not immediately answer, walking past Quinn to the stairs that led up to the bedroom. "Angel?"

Angel paced once inside the sanctum of his bedroom, taking in slow deep breaths to calm his rising blood pressure. The new meds were still taking effect. It wasn't even *his* room. It was a room he shared with Quinn, just like the other master suite was a room he shared with Rachel. It occurred to him then that he had no space that was *just* his.

He sat heavily on the bed, flexing his hand while practicing his breathing. He was too worked up. He wanted to hit someone or something out of pure, unadulterated rage. The Langs were so infuriating!

"Angel?" Quinn asked, hovering at the bedroom door. "You ok?"

Angel didn't answer. He shifted to an Indian-style position instead, taking in a deep breath.

"Angel?" Quinn prodded.

"Pretty sure your mom is still standing on the porch."

"What?!"

"I told her she wasn't welcome here," Angel continued, eyes still closed, fist opening and closing in a vain attempt to get his temper under control. "I'm done, Quinn. I'm not pandering to their bullshit anymore and neither are you. They're not going to bully you into doing what *they* think is best for their social status. They're not going to do it to Gage or Mackenzie either, and they're certainly not going to keep blaming me like *I'm* the villain of this story. I'm over it. It's done. Next time they get a police escort off the property."

Angel let out a little huff after his spew of words. The other man remained silent. Their room no longer felt like a monstrous cavern, like it did the first couple weeks of living there. They opted for fun, whimsical decor and lots of second-hand finds that added a touch of boho chic. The entire townhouse felt that way – lived in and loved. It even smelled nice, filled with oil diffusers that carried the soft scent of lavender and sage throughout the fifty-three hundred square feet of marble and wood. The rug beneath the bed had a subtle damask pattern on it that caught his eye once he deigned to open them, and held him enraptured until Quinn touched his shoulder.

"You ok?" Quinn asked, looking like he'd asked more than once. Angel nodded.

"I'm sorry, Angel."

"For what?" Angel asked. He sounded tired, felt it too.

"For everything," Quinn answered, wrapping him up in a warm embrace, letting Angel lean in for support. "For freaking out and ruining what we had."

"I like what we have now," Angel assured. He meant it too. His heart was so full with Quinn and Rachel in his life, with Mackenzie and Gage and even Rachel's stupid Chihuahua. Hell, he even liked having Sofia around to help out and speak Spanish to – the young woman was surprisingly fluent in all the Latin languages. Their life wasn't perfect and *that* was the most perfect thing in the world for Angel. "She's still at the door, isn't she?"

Quinn pulled his phone out, opening the Ring app, and sighed. "Back door, actually. I should talk to her."

"I'll go too. I don't mind telling her where to stick it," Angel said. Quinn laughed.

"I love you so much," the Asian man said.

Angel smiled. "I love you too."

The moment was ruined by the buzzing of Quinn's phone due to the security system being triggered. Both men looked at each other and groaned.

"She's tenacious," Angel grumbled.

"No shit," Quinn sighed, helping Angel to his feet. He wobbled his way out of the room, suddenly aware of the minor seizure he must have had to warrant the concern Quinn displayed earlier. These people were going to kill him by mere presence alone!

#

Not to be deterred from her mission, Marjorie Lang walked around the entire property until finding what she wanted – a key under the back door mat. The basement apartment smelled like stale Chinese food and wet socks. Her nose wrinkled in disgust. The furnishings were paltry, the decor a sad myriad of unframed posters and toys meant to look like little demons or something equally terrifying. Their heads were too big for the small bodies. The stairs out of the apartment were too narrow and steep, made of creaking wood and a pipe in place of a proper handrail.

"Atrocious," she muttered. "Nothing nice about this place at all."

"Mom?" Marjorie came up short as soon as she heard the voice speaking to her. Gage. "What the hell are you doing here?"

"Getting this family back on track, Gage Nicholas Lang!" she hissed. "I've had it with your brother's nonsense. That unwashed miscreant he's embroiled himself in has ruined all of his good sense and dragged this family through the mud. I won't stand for it any longer, Gage. And I won't tolerate it from you either. You're coming home immediately."

"Hard pass," Gage said stepping away from her like she was diseased. If anything was diseased, it was the hovel he was living in!

"Gage, I said I was done with this nonsense. Pack. Your. Things."

"Gage isn't going anywhere, Mrs. Lang," Angel said as he and Quinn came down the narrow, rickety stairs into the basement level. "You, however, are or *I* will be calling the police."

"Well, I never! Quinn! Honestly, is this any way to treat your mother? What kind of *mooch* do you have living with you!"

"Excuse me–" Angel started, but Quinn cut him off, tucking the taller man behind him in a comical display of chivalry. Marjorie felt sick to her stomach, watching them.

"Angel is my *partner*, mom," Quinn said in a tone that Marjorie did not appreciate at all. "He's not mooching off anyone. He's on leave because Mackenzie needs *both* of us around right now *and* because Gage *poisoned* him and it has affected his health."

"Don't be absurd, Quinn, your brother–"

"Did what *Willow* asked him to do. *Willow,*

mom. Because he was more afraid of *you and dad* than prison. We don't want your money. We don't want your status or any of your crap. *I* want Angel. *I* want to be left alone," Quinn started, taking in a deep breath before finally adding, "I want you to leave my house. *Our* house."

Marjorie felt her lips pursing together in a tight pucker of barely suppressed rage. Not a single word of what Quinn said made any sense. The two *lied* about their engagement, made a mockery of everything that had been done for them in front of the entire community. If Larry was to be believed, Angel not only carried on in a relationship with Quinn, but with the fat girl that came as part of his very small and sad entourage. Marjorie didn't recall her name. It wasn't important.

"This is absolutely unacceptable, Quinn. We have given you *everything*," Marjorie said. Quinn shook his head.

"You're right," Angel said, stepping out from behind Quinn to wrap his arm around Marjorie's son. "You gave him every ounce of self-loathing he has. You gave Gage and Elliott addiction habits so profound they both literally ran from you to get clean. Gage is doing really well here. I wish I could have said the same for Elliott."

"Don't you dare speak about my son, Mr. Rivera," Marjorie hissed. Tears stung her eyes just *thinking* about the awfulness that took Elliott from them. "My son…"

"Was an alcoholic," Angel continued. "One who recognized it and wanted to get help. Did you encourage it? Or did you just tell him how shameful it would be if anyone found out?"

Marjorie gaped. Angel merely nodded. "I think it's time for you to go, Mrs. Lang," Angel finished. Marjorie felt the rage roil in her gut.

"I'll walk you out," Quinn said, guiding her up and out through the main level by her elbow like some sort of criminal, paraded in front of the fat girl and Mackenzie on her way to the front door.

"Quinn!" Marjorie blubbered.

"Bye, mom."

"Quinn Anthony Lang, stop this right now! This is absurd! You owe it to us to make reparations for what you've pulled! Quinn!" she screeched as the door slammed in her face for a second time.

22

The subdued cacophony of many voices filled the open space around Rachel and Angel. She demanded that they remove the foul taste Marjorie Lang left in their mouths by going for some retail therapy. All of them. She and Angel sat on a bench in the middle of the mall while Quinn retrieved some snacks. Gage, Sofia, and Mackenzie had already run off to the stores with all the latest tech and games. Rachel let them. Gage needed to spend as much time with his niece as the three of them did and seemed to be crushing on Sofia pretty hard, too. It was cute. It was also a Herculean effort to make sure that Mackenzie knew she was wanted, loved, and safe – things they knew she never had with her parents. In fact, the only thing Paige Lang argued about was where the money was going. The will left it all to Mackenzie, held in trust by Quinn until her sixteenth birthday. Absolutely no one in the Lang hierarchy was happy with that decision. Even Bella made her opinions known on that one, resulting in Quinn's first broken phone.

"Ok, what about that guy?" Rachel asked, pointing to a man that wore pink shorts and a polo. He was handsome, tall, blonde.

"Meh," Angel shrugged. Rachel laughed. Angel laughed too. "Why are you asking if I think they're cute? Do you?"

"I don't know, some of them are. Just... kinda curious, which you look at more," Rachel said. She had been *immensely* curious but too afraid to come out and ask it. In fact, Quinn had been curious, too. Angel's seizures, while blessedly reducing, gave Rachel and Quinn ample opportunity to talk and get to know each other a little better than just 'Angel's Bookends'. Several of their friends had already given Rachel and Quinn that odd term of endearment. No one truly seemed to have an issue with their arrangement, however, which was surprising.

"I don't," Angel shrugged, looking at Rachel. "I don't really have reason to."

Rachel felt herself flushing. The goofy grin Angel gave her did not help alleviate the red rising in her face in the least.

"Why's Rachel all red?" Quinn asked as he returned, sitting on the other side of Angel. Definitely his bookends.

"I told her I don't need to look at other people – male or female," Angel said. He took one of the pretzels Quinn bought as well as the enormously sized lemonade the three were meant to share.

"While looking at *me*," Rachel added, still trying to hide her face. The whole mall was probably looking at her now. "I mean, am I the reason you don't look or …"

"Well, yeah. I have you," Angel said, kissing her head. "And Quinn. I don't need to look at anyone else."

"That's horseshit, you didn't look at anyone before any of this happened," Quinn pointed out while biting into his pretzel. "Me included."

"Quinn, I looked at you everyday. I lived with you. *Still* live with you. I think there's been like, a total of two weeks max that I have *not* looked at you in some capacity. I saw you naked before I saw Rachel naked."

"While that is all true," Quinn continued. "That was because we were roommates and that is not the same thing. You have not looked at anyone else *but* Rachel in that romantic, 'so hot I need to fuck them' way until recently when you've added me. Still processing that, by the way, because I swear I think you're looking at someone behind me or something when you do that."

Angel laughed again. Rachel felt better knowing that Quinn noticed it, too. It was a small wonder she got him to notice *her*. Honestly, if it hadn't been for that awful day on the Metro, he may not have looked at all. They'd already worked together for a whole year before that incident.

"Why does it matter if I look at other people or not?" Angel asked, nibbling on his pretzel. "Do you guys want to look? I won't stop you. Watch, that guy over there Q, with the pink shorts. Hot or not?"

"Ok, first, pink shorts should never be a thing," Quinn answered. Rachel laughed at that. Angel chuckled too, shoulders moving silently as he tried not to bust out like Rachel knew he wanted to. "Shush. Never a thing. Second... not. The pink shorts killed it."

"Since when do you care about *fashion*?" Angel finally snorted through his laughter. Quinn blinked at him. "Fine, ok, no pink shorts. What about her?"

"That's problem number one, she's a *her*. Not really my thing, remember?" Quinn said. "I like her shirt though."

The woman wore a classic Jurassic Park shirt. Of course, Quinn liked it. It screamed geek. The point was made. Quinn didn't have any attraction to women. Rachel could live with that. Angel was the one she needed to figure out – for her sake and Quinn's.

"You really don't look at anyone at all?" she dared to ask, nibbling on her pretzel. Angel shook his head.

"I told you. I don't have reason to look. Not even out of curiosity. Just gets a bunch of glares from people anyway in my experience," Angel answered. Rachel simply giggled and left it at that. She threw Quinn a knowing look, glad to see the man catching on quickly.

Angel was theirs, and theirs alone.

#

It took several weeks, one too many bottles of wine, and an excessive amount of sex to really get over Marjorie Lang's abrupt intrusion into their lives, even if the immediate mall trip that followed helped some. It was all just too much for Quinn to handle. He wondered at one point if he was going to turn into a raging alcoholic like his siblings and quickly set the bottle aside after that. He didn't look at it again. Angel's medication was finally taking effect, reducing his seizures to minimal annoyances rather than nearly–catastrophic, life–

altering events. Rachel put the entire household on a strict, mostly vegetarian diet for Angel's benefit, and made everyone – Gage included – go for an evening walk after dinner. In fact, the relationship Quinn had with his brother was probably the most surprising thing to come out of the absolute chaos that was Quinn's existence.

"Ok, so don't be nervous. Remember to smile and wait until I'm *not* visible to ask him. Ok?" Gage said, fixing Quinn's shirt so it sat right on his shoulders.

Quinn took in a deep breath and nodded. He and Angel had had a long discussion after his mother's invasion of their life. Quinn had fallen into a bad place again, full of doubt and worry that all came to a head when he told Angel in very short, unintelligible words to just marry Rachel and forget about Quinn. And, while Angel assured him that such a thing would *not* be happening, he did ask if it was ok to marry Rachel too. It was Angel's wish for the three of them to form what he called a 'throuple'.

Initially Quinn receded further into himself but, after a twenty-four-hour mope fest, and a swift boot to the head from Gage, he pulled his head out of his ass and agreed to what Angel wanted. Quinn even helped Angel pick a ring for Rachel. He hadn't seen it on her finger yet, however, so assumed Angel hadn't asked yet.

That was neither here nor there. Now, it was Quinn's turn to finally and officially ask Angel to marry *him*. He wanted to puke.

"Hey," Gage said, smacking Quinn's face lightly. "Don't look so green. It'll be fine. You're gonna kill it."

"That's not helping," Quinn sighed.

"Fine, make it a game. You have to win over the big boss to get laid or else you start over on the couch," Gage offered. Quinn threw a flat glare at him.

"What is it with you people turning everything into some weird new game?"

Gage shrugged. "You understand it better than real life, dude."

Quinn just glowered. Gage beamed, gave him a big thumbs up, and moved out of sight in the kitchen just as the front door opened.

"...to just do one match, but Mrs. Clay said we couldn't bring our game systems to school, so she took them! It's not fair!" Mackenzie said, her voice echoing through the vast marble expanse in which they lived.

"Well, she's not wrong. School isn't for video game matches," Angel explained with all the patience of a slow-moving glacier. He absolutely adored Mackenzie, which made Quinn love him even more. Then more again when Angel came over to give him a kiss as he brought Mackenzie in for her after-school snack. Sofia left the small applesauce pouch with a cute note for Mackenzie before going out to get groceries for dinner. The Italian nanny loved Mackenzie as much as Quinn and Angel did.

"Hi, Uncle Quinn."

"Hey, kiddo," Quinn replied. He still could not look at his niece without thinking of Elliott. They'd never been close, barely spoke more than once a year, yet *Quinn* was the one Elliott trusted most with Mackenzie's well-being. It was mind-boggling. It was also not something Quinn needed to be thinking about. He glanced over at where Gage hid, getting a 'go on' gesture from his little brother. "Hey, uhm, can you go check on Juju for me?"

"The dog or the plant?" Mackenzie asked. Quinn blinked.

"Both?"

Mackenzie giggled, grabbed her squeezable applesauce, and moved on to do as she was asked. Angel watched her go, smiling at Quinn.

"She got her Switch taken away today at school," Angel explained. "We get our first parent-teacher conference about it tomorrow."

"Oh..." Quinn said, slightly derailed by that.

He forced himself to focus, to think about the game – about getting laid – and nodded. "Y–yeah, we can do that."

"You ok? You seem nervous," Angel asked as he went to the fridge, digging through it for something. Quinn looked at Gage again. Gage's eyes widened in encouragement, the young man mouthing 'now'. Quinn nodded and fished the tiny ring out of his pocket.

He'd actually 'dressed up' for this, putting on clean jeans and a shirt that didn't have holes in it. In fact, he looked down to make sure it didn't have holes. It had a stylized bowl of ramen on it, but no holes. As soon as Angel came up from behind the fridge door, Quinn stuck the ring out.

"Marry me?" he blurted. Out of the corner of his eye, he caught sight of Gage smacking himself in the forehead. Angel, however, blinked at him.

"What?" he chuckled. "Q..."

Quinn shut the fridge door, took in a big breath, and let it out slowly as he got down on one knee. "I know I sort of already asked, but then things got way messed up. I don't think I understand what all of this is still. Maybe I don't want to. I know I *want* to spend the rest of my life with you. I always have. Will you spend the rest of your life with me, Angel? Will you marry me?"

It all came out mostly as a ramble of words

and crazy emotions. Quinn's heart slammed in his chest so hard he was finding it difficult to breathe, and he was sure Angel could hear it. He wouldn't look at Angel, though. He couldn't, as if expecting mockery or rejection.

"Yes," Angel replied. Now Quinn looked up. Tears ran down Angel's face, over the rounded cheeks of a barely surprised smile of delight as he nodded and repeated, "Yes."

Relief flooded Quinn so much that his head spun as he stood, toppling him into Angel from the *massive* head rush it caused. Angel caught him, holding him close while chuckling a little.

"Head rush?" he asked. Quinn nodded, then winced, feeling his face burn with embarrassment. The head rush cleared in seconds, but the rush of red to his face didn't.

"S-sorry. Uhm..." Quinn said, then lifted the ring up. It was a titanium band with a row of tiny diamonds inlaid inside the band. At the center was a larger diamond, placed flat in the setting. Gage helped him pick it out. "Marry me? Again?"

Angel laughed but nodded, his eyes squinting up to half-moon slits. "Yes, I'll marry you."

Quinn smiled too, sliding the ring onto Angel's finger. As soon as Quinn saw it there, any anxiety he felt melted. He took hold of Angel's face and kissed him deep and long, heart soaring.

23

ngel savored the time he had with
Quinn. He was soaring on a cloud
of bliss, heart full, and mind at peace. He lay
beside Quinn, the late afternoon sun beginning its
descent into the horizon. School just started for
Mackenzie, but she was already proving how hard
parenthood was. Gage took the girl to meet Sofia
so Angel and Quinn could have some privacy, for
which Angel was grateful.

"I love you," Angel said, running his fingers
along the length of Quinn's arm. He kissed the
back of Quinn's neck and shoulder. They'd been
going at it since the proposal, lost in the euphoria
of this tiny slice of bliss they were living in.

Quinn glanced over his shoulder and smiled.
"I love you too, Angel. God, you have no idea how
much I love you."

"Then show me," Angel encouraged, nuzzling into Quinn's neck. Quinn rolled to face Angel, smiling in a way that Angel had come to love in the last few months. It was a wicked grin, a playful grin that promised a side of Quinn that only Angel or Rachel got to see. He was submissive in every other aspect of his life, but in the bedroom, he dominated any chance he got. Rachel found it amusing, especially on the evenings when *Quinn* asked her to join so he could top *and* watch live porn – or so Quinn said. Angel never complained and willingly gave in to Quinn's whims.

"Show you?" Quinn repeated in a husky whisper that sent a thrill through Angel's whole body. Angel smiled, encouraging Quinn to be bold. He got his wish.

Quinn kissed his way down Angel's torso in a sensual tease that had Angel's toes curling and cock throbbing before Quinn even came remotely close to that area. When Quinn finally *did* come close to his crotch, Angel thought he might lose his mind. The man was a *very* quick study. Angel knew he watched porn. They *all* watched porn. It had become a Tuesday night pastime since moving in together. The goal was to find the most ludicrous piece of pornography on the internet. The benefits after were well worth any stupidity they stumbled upon.

That was Angel's foremost thought as Quinn took him in his mouth. Then, all thought ceased. Everything Quinn did sent a shiver through him, drew out a low moan and made his body writhe with need.

"Oh God, Quinn..." Angel breathed, fingers tangled in Quinn's dark hair. Quinn took it as encouragement, giving Angel more, sucking deeper, teasing Angel's pucker. So far it had been Angel topping. Now it was Quinn's turn and Angel was practically ready to scream at the man to ravage him. "Quinn!"

The man's name was drawn from Angel's throat with a desperate squeak that had him giving a spurt of cum into Quinn's throat before Quinn pinched off the rest of the orgasm and came up off of Angel's cock.

"Not yet," he purred, kissing Angel's thigh, move down further to give Angel the best rim job he'd ever had, again drawing him so close to the edge he wanted to scream before stopping abruptly. "I love those noises you make."

"You suck," Angel whined, covering his face with a pillow.

"I was, yeah," Quinn teased, pressing himself to Angel's entrance. "You wanted me to show you how much I love you."

Angel did scream then, screamed in

euphoric bliss as Quinn entered him. He was slick with lube and slid right in to the hilt. He felt Quinn bend forward, and forced himself to breathe even as Quinn removed the pillow from his face.

"Someone likes that," Quinn teased. He moved slowly, rocking with Angel rather than anything frantic. It felt amazing.

"I hate you a little," Angel whined, sucking in a sharp breath when Quinn kissed him. The man literally took Angel's breath away, making love to him in the most amazing way possible. Every stroke, every movement, every little twitch made Angel want to cry out until he finally did, practically roaring into Quinn's mouth as he orgasmed. Quinn followed shortly thereafter, filling him with a warmth Angel could never get enough of.

Angel breathed a low whimper into their kiss, holding Quinn tight while still reeling from the euphoria of what they just shared. Quinn returned the kiss, with the passion and love that Angel could feel in how he was held, in what they had just done, in the pounding of his heart and Quinn's.

"God, I love you," Angel finally breathed, brow pressed to Quinn's. "So much."

"Same," Quinn replied. He got quiet after. Quiet in the way Angel knew meant he was overthinking things.

"What's wrong?"

"Nothing," Quinn replied with the speed of a lightning bolt. He even sighed after because he realized how stupid it sounded. "I dunno, thinking, I guess."

"About?" Angel prodded gently, rubbing Quinn's back. Quinn just sighed again and laid his head on Angel's chest, their legs intertwined. "Q?"

"Can I have sex with Rachel?" he blurted. Angel blinked at the top of Quinn's head, feeling the tension in his fiance's muscles.

"You… want to have sex with Rachel?" Angel asked, needing the clarification more than anything. Quinn didn't *like* women. They'd found that to be abundantly clear anytime they went out.

"Nevermind," Quinn said as quickly as he said 'nothing'.

"Q? Why don't you ask *her*?"

Quinn looked up at him with a frown. "Cuz she's *your* girlfriend."

The logistics of their relationship were still a little odd to them. What to call each other, what boundaries were safe and what was off limits. It was a learning curve for all of them, but they'd been managing it well – or so Angel thought.

"That doesn't mean she's *mine*. I just… I dunno, I guess we both just figured you weren't at all interested."

"I'm not. I'm... I mean I *am* but not like you think, I just... I'm curious, ok? The last time I had sex with a girl was when I was *seventeen*, Angel. I'm pretty sure we didn't do *anything* right, and she was mean anyway. You always look like you really enjoy it when we have sex together with her. So... I was just kinda curious, is all. Forget I said anything. It's stup–"

Angel silenced Quinn with a deep, long kiss. At the very least, it succeeded in relaxing all of Quinn's muscles. The man literally melted right into Angel's chest and arms, even moaning softly into the kiss.

"Ask her," Angel encouraged, still close enough to Quinn for him to feel Angel's lips move against his.

"Really? You don't mind?" Quinn mumbled. Angel grinned, shaking his head.

"I don't mind. I think I may love you even more for it, for including her, for being adorable enough to worry about it," Angel smiled. Quinn's ears turned red. That was all it took for Angel to kiss him again, initiating another round of love-making between them.

#

Rachel narrowed her eyes, scanning the top of the table for the next piece of the puzzle. Gage sat with her, digging through the pieces spread out before them for specific types. She got off work early, hoping to catch the guys before they had to deal with Mackenzie's conference about her Switch. The Metro ran over forty minutes behind, however. They were gone by the time she got home.

"Think it's going ok?" Gage asked. Music played throughout the first level. It was one of the extras that Quinn put money into – a whole–house sound system. He'd also talked her and Angel into installing an intercom system too. The install was scheduled for the following week. The whole house was a little over the top for her liking, but she wasn't going to complain too much. Each of them had their own space. They each had a say in what went into the communal spaces, and everyone took a turn making dinner. She instituted a strict diet for all of them to better help Angel, as well as an evening stroll for the same reason. The Lang brothers complained for the first week, then Angel convinced her to loosen up a bit on the diet. They had a quiet life full of love and understanding. Mostly.

"I'm sure it is. They can handle a conference," Rachel assured him, even if she had her own doubts. *Angel* could handle a conference; Quinn might actually faint. She was surprised he had the constitution to propose to Angel – and was a little jealous that Angel had not proposed to *her*. Logistically, she knew there could only be *one* legally binding marriage between them, but it was the principle of it. Rachel had asked Angel first.

Speaking of the Devil summoned him, and the same was true for Quinn and Angel. The two walked in with Mackenzie shortly after her brooding, jealousy-laden thought. Mackenzie pouted right past the living room where Gage and Rachel were working on the puzzle, heading straight for her room. Rachel looked at the boys next. Quinn pouted too, walking into his office, shutting the door with a soft click.

"Uh oh," Rachel prompted, looking to Angel, the only one *not* pouting. "That bad?"

Angel shrugged. "Quinn had to ground her. He doesn't like being mean."

"That's not mean. She took a game system to school," Rachel pointed out. Gage stayed pointedly silent.

"I know. That's what I said. He still thinks he's being mean," Angel sighed. He came to sit beside her on the couch, looking at the puzzle. It took less than thirty seconds for him to find the piece *Rachel* had been looking for. She glared at him.

"What?" he asked, noticing her glare. Of course, he noticed. The man hyper-focused on most things but remained oblivious to others.

"Nothing. I've been looking for that piece for, like, twenty minutes," she said, letting her annoyance show. He kissed her head.

"You did all the hard work for me," he soothed. She hated when he did that. Mostly because it made her turn into a puddle.

"I'm gonna go check on Mackie," Gage said. They both nodded at him, watching him head up to the second floor.

"I'm gonna grab some wine. You want some?" Rachel asked as she stood up. Initially, she was going to wait until dinner, but something told her dinner was going to be a little unconventional.

"Wine sounds good. Sofia out?"

"Yeah. She's getting Mackie more school clothes," Rachel said as she pulled two glasses from their rack. There was a small wine bar as well as a coffee station in their kitchen. Their stove was gas, their refrigerator was smart, even the dishwasher had a phone app that told them when the cycle was done. Again, a little over the top for her tastes, but she was growing more fond of the things in the house meant to make life easier. She opened a new bottle of wine, one of Angel's favorites, and brought the two glasses and bottle back to the living room.

"Maybe we can just do a carving board for... dinner..." Rachel said, her words slowing when she saw the tiny box on the table. Inside it was a stunningly beautiful diamond ring. Angel continued looking for puzzle pieces, popping one in place before turning to look at her with an angelic smile on his face. He stood up, took the wineglasses from her hand and set them down, then took the wine bottle. He set that down too, grabbing the box after.

Rachel felt her heart slam inside of her chest and her stomach tighten. She knew this should not bring on a panic attack, yet she felt like all the air was rushing out of her lungs all the same, *especially* when Angel got down on one knee.

"I know I should've done this sooner or made a bigger deal of it, but it just didn't feel right. It doesn't matter. What does matter is how much I love you; how much I need you in my life. Rachel, will you grow old with me as my wife?"

The panic turned to joy that turned into tears that ran down her face. She must have looked a complete mess. She could not have asked for anything more perfect than what Angel just gave her. They were not fancy people; they didn't throw wild parties or plan epic events. They were happy to exist with a box of Cheez–Its and wine coolers on a Goodwill–bought couch. She loved that more than she realized as she stood there nodding like a fool.

"Yes," she forced herself to say. "Yes, I'll grow old with you."

Angel smiled up at her, standing so he could put the ring on her finger. Rachel threw her arms around his neck, kissing him soundly. He wrapped his arms around her, returning the kiss, swaying in time to the music.

#

Quinn fussed around in the kitchen with Mackenzie shadowing him after dinner. It was his night to do dishes. He rinsed and Mackenzie loaded. They had a system, a tiny routine that worked well for them. He made a deal with her: she would help with dishes for a week and then he would buy her a new Switch. The school kept hers until the end of the school year, which was absurd. Quinn told Angel it was militant. Angel reminded him that it was a private school, they were allowed to be militant.

Angel proposed to Rachel while Quinn was pouting. He wasn't sure how to feel about it. Logically, he knew it was coming, but his anxiety–driven emotions fed him seeds of doubt and jealousy. Those doubts festered until well after Mackenzie was in bed and the house was quiet. He heard splashing in the pool and let his weary feet lead him out to the back where Angel and Rachel splashed around.

"Hey Q!" Rachel giggled as if he were the punch line of some inside joke. "Come join us!"

"I'm ok," Quinn lied. He knew he wasn't ok.

"Come on, Quinn. Please?" Angel asked. Quinn shook his head, moving to sit in one of the nearby chairs. "What's wrong, Quinn?"

"Nothing."

Angel threw him a look, glanced back at Rachel, then got out of the pool. Quinn didn't want to talk about his crazy, messed up head. Angel played shrink far too often, encouraging him to go to a real one. Quinn didn't like that idea much. Shrinks just made people feel worse by pointing out all the flaws. However, Angel didn't come to talk. Instead, the lunatic picked Quinn up like a sack of potatoes and jumped back into the pool.

"Angel! What the crap!" Quinn spluttered. He still had all his clothes on!

"No more pouting. We're having fun and celebrating. Because we're happy, Quinn. Happy. Our family is awesome, your brother is sober and doing so well at school, Mackie is an amazing kid. And..." Angel said, still holding on to Quinn's saturated shirt. "We're getting married."

Quinn tried to argue, but Angel silenced him with a kiss that took all his worries away.

"You could've warned me," Quinn whined, silenced again with another kiss.

"And spoil the fun?" Angel teased. Rachel giggled, watching them. "You could ask her now, you know."

"Ask her what?" Quinn replied.

"If you two can have sex, Q."

Quinn's face flushed bright red. If he was being honest, he'd forgotten about that request. He rather hoped Angel had too. Clearly, the man had not forgotten.

"I don't wanna ask her now. That's...weird."

"Do you want me to ask her?" Angel said.

"No!" Quinn hissed. "Have you been drinking?"

"Yes. Rae," Angel said.

"Angel, don't!"

"What's up?" Rachel said, swimming over to them. Quinn realized then that they were both naked and felt his face grow hotter.

"Quinn wants to have sex with you," Angel said. Blunt. To the point. Embarrassing as fuck.

"Really?" she giggled in disbelief. Quinn wanted to drown himself. "Wait, for real? You do?"

"It was just a thought," Quinn muttered. "It's not a big deal."

"Quinn, you don't like women. It's a big deal," Rachel said, then hugged him tight. Quinn was not expecting any form of affection and froze.

"Uhm..."

"Of course we can!"

"Ok..." Quinn replied, uncertainty clear in his voice. His uncertainty was made worse by feeling Angel kissing on his neck while tugging his soaking sweatpants off. "N-not now!"

"Relax, Q," Angel said, sending the sweats floating away. Quinn's shirt followed, making a loud slapping sound when it hit the surface of the water.

Quinn was the opposite of relaxed. He was a wire spring ready to snap. And sporting a boner to boot. Because of course he was. Angel was the only one who could do that without even trying.

"How much did you drink?" Quinn dared while Angel covered his neck in kisses.

"A bit," Angel murmured. His hands ran up and down Quinn's chest in ways that made Quinn shiver. Rachel smiled at him, still very close. Panic seized every part of Quinn until Rachel closed the space between them and kissed him.

Fuck it... Quinn thought, kissing her back as if she were Angel.

Her lips were softer, fuller, and more inviting. She guided his hands to her breasts, encouraging play. Quinn was positive none of this would be happening if Angel were not behind him making him feel good. But, all things considered, Rachel's breasts were nice. They felt like heavy pillows.

She parted his lips gently with her tongue,

deepening the kiss. Quinn let her, trying to enjoy the moment and not over-think it. He'd watched Angel have sex with Rachel plenty of times now. It turned him on a lot to watch them while Quinn took Angel from behind. Angel sandwiches, they called it. This was no different, except now Quinn was the meat. He had to remind himself of that at least three times before his panic started to abate. Which, of course, was around the time Angel decided to slip an exploratory finger into Quinn's ass.

Quinn gasped, then moaned into the kiss. Tag-teaming hardly seemed fair! How would he know if he enjoyed any part of sex with Rachel if *Angel* was making him feel good too?

"Make her feel good, Quinn," Angel purred into his ear, fingering Quinn only long enough to make sure Quinn was *really* horny. The man then floated along beside them, kissing them both before moving behind Rachel to kiss her neck and shoulders. Quinn had about as much experience with women as he did in brain surgery, but he was an avid porn watcher, so he started there, grabbing Rachel by the hips to bring her to him, lifting her legs up around his waist as he entered her.

To Quinn's delight, Rachel moaned into their kiss. And, much like their kiss, she was soft and warm inside. His hands slid back up to her breasts as soon as Rachel hooked her legs around him, arms around his neck as she moved with him in the water. Quinn's breathing increased as he thrust into her, slowly, grinding with her, using her own motions to guide him. It felt better than he expected. Not as good as it did with Angel, but he could see enjoying it from time to time.

"God, Quinn," Rachel mewled against his lips, squeezing her legs tighter around him. Her warm walls squeezed tighter too, making Quinn shiver. "Please keep going. Please..."

Quinn had not stopped, but he increased his thrusting, sliding his hands down to her ass to give it a squeeze. He could feel Angel pressed against her, the man's chest giving her support as he kissed her neck. Quinn reached for his partner, his fiancé, his everything. Angel took Quinn's hand and brought it to his lips. Quinn watched him, smiling as he thrust into Rachel. She had her head buried in Quinn's shoulder, riding him pretty hard, thighs squeezing tight.

"I need you," Quinn whispered to Angel. Angel smiled at him, leaning in to kiss Quinn while he had sex with Rachel. It was quite possibly one of the most amazing things Quinn had ever felt. He felt loved and wanted, sharing that with Angel, and with Rachel. He held her tight, kept Angel close to him, kissing him deep and long until Rachel cried out into his ear and gushed warmth all over Quinn's cock, tightening on him like a vice.

"F–fuck!" Quinn stammered, not expecting the sensation at all. *That* had certainly not happened the one and only time he'd had sex with a girl. He was instantly overcome with euphoria, shooting up into Rachel as his body spasmed, making her cry out again, clamping down harder. "Oh, shit, Rachel!"

"FUCK!" she cried out, throwing her head back, riding him through her orgasm. "Yes, Quinn!"

Angel joined them then, sliding into Quinn so slowly that all Quinn could do was shut his eyes tight in ecstasy. They stayed that way for what seemed like forever, all three of them sharing something new, reaching a new level of love and trust between the *three* of them that had Quinn's heart soaring.

ABOUT *The Author*

Noa Rose is a housewife, mother, and insane emotional stress baker during the day while moonlighting as an author of the intimate, divine, and taboo. Noa's first anthology publication was in Corrugated Sky's Insurgence: A Fae Rebellion Anthology. She has also self-published three short erotica pieces through Amazon.

Her alter ego, Michelle Schad, has four published books and several published short stories featuring LGBTQIA+, and diverse characters of all backgrounds. She shares her office with a few different decorative skulls to remind her of her wicked side, way too many Eeyore stuffies, three cats, and a dog suffering identity crisis.